"The bus comes," Artkin said.

Miro heard the slow screech of brakes as the bus stopped farther up the street. He craned his neck to look through the windshield and saw the orange vehicle a hundred yards away. He glanced at his watch. They would overtake the bus in seven minutes on a deserted stretch of road outside the town. In another twenty minutes, they would be at the bridge. Fifteen and seven were twenty-two. Allow three minutes for unexpected events. (Always allow, Artkin said repeatedly.) So, within twenty-five minutes, I will have killed my first man. A man will have died because of me.

But it turned out not to be a man.

Robert Cormier

AFTER THE FIRST DEATH

to my daughter Renée
with love

Published by
Dell Publishing
a division of
Bantam Doubleday Dell Publishing Group, Inc.
666 Fifth Avenue
New York, New York 10103

ISBN: 0-440-20835-1

RL: 6.2

Reprinted by arrangement with Pantheon Books, a division of Random House, Inc.

Printed in the United States of America

March 1991

10 9 8 7 6 5 4

RAD

After the first death,
there is no other.

DYLAN THOMAS

After the First Death

part
1

I keep thinking that I have a tunnel in my chest. The path the bullet took, burrowing through the flesh and sinew and whatever muscle the bullet encountered (I am not the macho-muscled type, not at five eleven and one hundred eighteen pounds). Anyway, the bullet went through my chest and out again. The wound has healed and there is no pain. The two ends of the tunnel are closed although there's a puckering of the skin at both ends of the tunnel. And a faint redness. The puckering has a distinct design, like the old vaccination scar on my father's arm. Years from now, the wound will probably hurt the way my father's old wounds hurt him, the wounds he received in those World War Two battles. My mother always jokes about the wounds: oh, not the wounds themselves but the fact that he professes to forecast weather by the phantom pains and throbbings in his arms and legs.

Will my wound ache like his when I am his age?

And will I be able to tell when the rain will fall by the pain whistling through the tunnel in my chest?

I am joking, of course, but my joking is entirely different from my mother's tender jokes.

I am joking because I won't have stayed around to become a human barometer or an instrument capable of forecasting weather.

But—who's the joke on?

The first of many questions about my presence here.

Keep a scorecard handy.

My father is scheduled to visit me today.

His first visit since the Bus and the Bridge last summer.

I am typing this in the room at Castle and it's beautiful here as I write this. Through the window, I can see the quadrangle and the guys indulging in a snowball fight. The first snowfall of the season. The snow is late this year. Christmas is only two weeks away. Thanksgiving was dry and cold with a pale sun in the sky but no wind. Perfect for a football game, the traditional game between Castle and Rushing Academy. Castle won, 21 to 6, and there was a big celebration on campus. Elliot Martingale brought these fireworks back from summer vacation; they were left over from July 4th at his family's place on Cape Cod, and he said they would be touched off when we won the big game on Thanksgiving Day. We won, he set them off. Beautiful. That's when I went to the john, swallowed fourteen sleeping pills, lay down on the bed listening to the cherry bombs explode and then a cluster of firecrackers going off like a miniature machine gun; and it was nice lying there, drifting away, and then I thought of the kids on the bus, strewn around like broken toys while the guns went off, and I started getting sick and rushed off to the bathroom to vomit.

Please do not consider these the notes of a self-pitying freak who needs the services of a psychiatrist.

I am not filled with pity for myself. And I'm not writing this to cop a plea of some kind.

I do not consider this a suicide note either.

Or even a prelude to one.

When the time comes to perform the act, I will do it without any prelude or prologue, and may simply walk up River Road one afternoon, arrive at Brimmler's Bridge, calmly climb the parapet or whatever it's called, and let myself plummet to the riverbed below.

I have deduced, reflecting on the Bus, that this would be the best way to shuffle off this mortal coil. Poetic justice, you see. Perhaps that's what I should have done when I was sent out to the Bus. The Bus was also on a bridge. That's when I should have taken the plunge, the dive, or the leap. The Bridge on which the Bus was perched is even higher than Brimmler's Bridge. Just think how I would have saved the day—and myself— that way.

And my father most of all.

But how many times is a person allowed to die?

Anyway, my parents are scheduled to arrive here late this morning.

Eleven o'clock to be exact.

My father's first visit since the Bus and the Bridge, but I already said that, didn't I?

My mother has been faithful about visiting. My mother is kind and witty and stylish. She is the essence of the loving wife and mother. She has such amazing strength, an inner strength that has nothing to do with the flexing of muscles. I always sensed it, even as a kid. My father has strength, too. But he has always been too shadowy to pin down. The nature of his profession, I realize now. His is the kind of profession that not only disguises the man but consumes him as well. And his family, too. Even my mother, with all her strength.

When she visited me the first time in September only a few days after my arrival, she played it cool and calm, and this is just what I needed.

"Do you want to talk about it, Mark?" she asked.

My name is Ben, my father's name is Mark. If it had been anyone but her, I would have called it a Freudian slip. But she is too uncomplicated for that kind of thing.

I wondered how much she knew about what happened on the bridge. "I'd rather not talk about it," I said. "Not just yet."

"Fine," she said, matter-of-factly, settling down for the visit, arranging her dress over her knees. She has beautiful legs and she is utterly feminine. She never wears slacks or pants suits, always skirts or dresses, even when she does housecleaning. She asked me about school and the classes and the guys, and I told her, talking mechanically, as if my mouth had nothing to do with the rest of my body. I told her about Mr. Chatham, who is my math teacher and might have taught my father a generation ago. This is one of the benefits of attending your father's alma mater, my mother said, when she drove me up here last fall. She said I would be able to gather new insights on my father. I didn't tell her that Mr. Chatham is practically senile, the butt of a thousand boyish and not-so-boyish pranks and jokes, and that he didn't remember my father at all. I had suggested the possibility to him. "My name is Ben Marchand," I'd told him, "and my father came to Castle back before World War Two—do you remember him?"

"Of course, dear boy," he said, "of course."

But I did not believe him. His eyes were glazed and vacant, his hand shook, and he always seems about to leap out of harm's way. Which is reflex action. Guys like Elliot Martingale and Biff Donateli rejoice in making old Chatham's last days lively. We keep him on his toes, keep him sharp, keep him from dropping into complete senility, Elliot says. How can a man drop out when he thinks a cherry bomb's going to go off in his pants any minute?

Anyway, I started to lie to my mother about Mr. Chatham and his nonexistent memories of my father. "He remembers Dad as a good student," I said. "Serious. Never fooled around much in class. A shy, sensitive lad: those were his exact words." I tried to imitate Mr. Chatham's rusty old voice: "A little too thin for his height, lad, but you could see he would fill out someday and be an outstanding man."

I could see immediately that she didn't believe me. She has many admirable qualities but she would never succeed as an actress. The disbelief was apparent in her eyes and in the expression on her face.

"Isn't Dad sensitive and wasn't he a good student?" I asked. "He must have been. He's a general now, isn't he?"

"You know your father doesn't like to be called a general," she said.

"True," I said, and felt myself drifting away from her, something I have been doing recently, drifting away while standing still, letting myself go as if the world is a huge blotter and I am being absorbed by it. "But he is a general, isn't he?" I asked, persisting, suddenly not wanting to drift away, not at this particular moment, wanting to make a point. What point?

And then my mother's strength asserted itself. "Ben," she said, her voice like the snapping of a tree branch. It reminded me of old movies on television where someone is screaming hysterically and someone else slaps the screamer and the hysterics die down. Well, I wasn't screaming hysterically but I must admit that I was hysterical all right. You can be hysterical without screaming or ranting and raving, or hitting your head against a wall. You can be quietly hysterical sitting in a dorm talking to your mother, watching the September sun climbing the wall like a ladder as it filters in through a sagging shutter. And the slap doesn't have to be a physical act; it can be one word, *Ben,* your own name lashing out. Yet she did it with love. I have always been assured of her love. And even as I responded to her shouted *Ben,* snapping me back from the drifting, I still said to myself: But he is a goddam general, whether he likes it or not, and that's why I'm here.

So we carried on a fairly normal conversation. About my classes, the guys: Yes, Mother, they're a good bunch. They leave me alone, mostly because I've come on the scene too late and it's hard to absorb me (they are not blotters, after all), but they are tactful, which surprises me really. I mean, Elliot Martingale is such a character with his clowning and all, and yet he came up to me the other day and said: "Marchand, old bastard, I looked up the back issues of the papers the other day and you're all right, know that?"

I felt either like bawling like a baby or laughing madly; either way, he'd think I was a complete nut. I felt like bawling because those were the first words anyone at Castle had said directly to me and they confirmed my existence here, something I was beginning to doubt. Until that moment, I might have been invisible or not there at all. And I felt like laughing madly because what Martingale said was so very wrong. What Elliot Martingale read about in the papers, my part in the Bus and the incident at the Bridge, was a million miles from the truth. Not lies exactly, of course. But information that was misleading, vague where it should be specific, specific where it should be vague. Inner Delta is very good at that sort of thing, of course.

There, I've said it: Inner Delta.
Like pulling a bandage off a festering sore.
Or a diseased rabbit from a soiled magician's hat.
Which, of course, is treason on my part, both as a son to my father and as a citizen of my country.

But do I really have a country?
And do I have citizenship anywhere?
I am a skeleton rattling my bones, a ghost laughing hollow up the sleeves of my shroud, a scarecrow whose straw is soaked with blood.

So much for the dramatics.
My name is Benjamin Marchand, son of Brigadier General and Mrs. Marcus L. Marchand. Although I am temporarily lodged at Castleton Academy in Pompey, New Hampshire, my home is at 1245 Iwo Jima Avenue, Fort Delta, Massachusetts.
Stick around. I may pass out picture postcards any moment now.

* * *

Those asterisks denote the passage of time. From 8:15 A.M. when I began typing this to the present moment: 10:46 A.M. Don't ask what I was doing those two and a half (more or less) hours.

But I'll tell you anyway.

After writing, I dressed and ran all the way up to Brimmler's Bridge, looked out at the frozen wasteland below, but decided for some perverse reason that I wanted to see my father before doing anything rash. Maybe I'm a masochist.

On the way back, I met Biff Donateli. He asked me if I would be joining the guys this evening in an excursion to the nearby domain of Pompey, where the amber of the gods would be quaffed by a select group of Knights. Knights of the Castle, get it? Anyway, Donateli talks like that—amber of the gods, for crissakes—although he looks like a thug, a hit man, dark and hairy.

The invitation stopped me in my tracks. I almost did a double take, like in the movies.

"Maybe," I said.

"That's the first complete sentence I've ever heard you utter," Donateli said, hustling away, his coat spotted with small explosions of snow from the snowball fight. I envied him. Those make-believe wounds.

Then I felt invisible again and looked to see if I actually left footprints behind me in the snow.

Back to that conversation with my mother.

A leftover, a postscript, maybe.

She said: "That description of your father. The way you described him to old Mr. Chatham. You realize you were describing yourself, don't you?"

"But Father, too?"
"You decide that, Ben."

On the desk near the window there's a Castle year-book. The year my father graduated. *Knights and Dayze*. I haven't looked at it yet. My father's picture is inside, of course, with the pictures of all his classmates, but I don't want to look at his picture. Not yet. I haven't seen him since the bridge because I don't want him seeing me. I'm afraid to even look at his picture because his eyes will be looking into mine. And I know I couldn't face those eyes even in a prep school yearbook.

I like that idea of picture postcards. Even verbal ones.
The first: Fort Delta.
An aeriel view. High up, like from a communication satellite: Fort Delta, located in almost the geographical center of New England. Closer view: barracks, post exchanges, residences, etc. All buildings the same, whether the Ulysses S. Grant Theater or the General John J. Pershing School I attended, all as alike and featureless as those houses and hotels you buy in Monopoly.

Delta is an ancient army post, with a history dating back to the Spanish-American War just before the turn of the century. I have no time to indulge in history and yet it's important to understand Delta in order to understand Inner Delta.

Fort Delta played its role through all the American wars—First World, Second World, Korea, Vietnam. And through the peace. As a processing center or a training ground for paratroopers and other specialists.

Home sweet home—that has always been Delta to me. There was a report a few years ago that Fort Delta would be closed down as an economy move. This came at a time when there was antiwar sentiment in the nation.

I approached my father, horrified.

If a kid lived in New York City, they couldn't close down New York, could they? Or Boston? Or even Hallowell, next door to Delta? But this was my home, where I played ball, went to school, to the movies, to the chapel twice a year at Christmas and Easter, where my father worked, where my mother was active in the Officers' Wives Association and planted her flowers and hung her clothes on the line in back of the house. How could they think of shutting this down?

Don't worry, Ben, my father had said.

But I worried anyway.

My father was right. Delta was not closed down and its activities were not curtailed in the slightest.

My father said: "See?" A note of quiet triumph in his voice.

Now I know what he knew and couldn't tell me. Fort Delta wasn't closed because of Inner Delta. Keeping Fort Delta open had nothing to do with the special Economic Impact Statement ordered by the Department of Defense or the Presidential Decree based on the Impact Statement. It had nothing to do with editorials written in the newspapers or speeches made by congressmen in Washington. Inner Delta was the key. Inner Delta was the tail that wagged the dog, that nobody knew about but a few people, my father among them. And Inner Delta was the reason I ended up on the bridge and why a bullet created a tunnel in my chest and why I dream of screaming children at night.

Another picture postcard: My father. A general who does not want to be a general.

My father, the patriot.

I only saw him in uniform that one time when he summoned me to his office. He wore the stars and stood behind the desk and for a moment I didn't recognize him. I had a feeling he wasn't my father at all, that my father had ceased to exist and an actor was taking his place, an old actor like Gregory Peck on old television movies. My father said: "Sit down, Benjamin." It was all very strange and formal because he never called me Benjamin and I had never been in his office before. I could feel my heart beating heavily, like a Chinese gong in my chest, because this was an important occasion. I knew little about his work except that it was secret and my mother and I were not supposed to ask questions. I knew, however, that his work was very special and separate from the regular Fort Delta routine. How did I know? Slips of the tongue. Phone calls I overheard. My father often spoke in a sort of code, but I cracked some of the code. Like, on the phone, he'd say: "Peripheral." After a while, I realized that meant I was around someplace, on the edges, and he wasn't free to talk.

I also knew the nature of his profession but not its details. Psychological stuff, behavior intervention, whatever that means. I ran across an old university journal in which he wrote out his theories and although the stuff was mostly double-talk to me, I noted the introduction in which he was described as a pioneer in his field, worthy perhaps of a Nobel Prize someday. To complete the portrait: my father was a professor at New England University in Boston before he accepted the commission and took my mother and me to Fort Delta when I was, like, three years old.

Anyway. I sat in the office and my father began to address me. Not talk to me but address me. As if I were not his son but a stranger who had suddenly become important to him. I hadn't connected my visit to the office with the bridge and the hostages until he began to talk. As he talked, I felt a drop of perspiration roll down from my armpit like a small cold marble. But at the same time I was happy and excited. Scared, too, of course, but somehow happy, knowing that I was suddenly a part of the secret life of my father.

No more room on this particular postcard.
Call it amnesia.
Emotional amnesia, maybe.
Or whatever the hell you wish.

Who the hell are you anyway, out there looking over my shoulder as I write this?
I feel you there, watching, waiting to get in.
Or is anybody there?

I once read the shortest horror story in the world. I don't know who wrote it.

It went something like this:

The last person on earth sat in a room.
There came a knock at the door.

Who will knock at my door?

When he arrives, will my father be wearing his uniform? Check One: Yes ＿＿ No ＿＿ Unsure ＿＿.
Will I be able to look him in the eye? Check One: Yes ＿＿ No ＿＿ Unsure ＿＿.
Will he be able to look me in the eye? Check One: No ＿＿ No ＿＿ No ＿＿

Maybe I should make another and final trip to Brimmler's Bridge before he arrives.

And take that sweet plummet into nothingness as the wind whistles through the tunnel in my chest and the hole in my heart.

part

2

Miro's assignment was to kill the driver. Without hesitation. As soon as the bus arrived at the bridge. Everyone must know without any delay that the takeover of the bus was critical, and that sudden death was fact not probability. When Miro was handed the revolver by Artkin, it felt heavy in his hand, although he had used the small automatic weapon countless times in target practice. But always a cardboard target. Now the target would be a human being. Miro swallowed with difficulty as he squeezed the barrel of the gun. The smell of the weapon, that peculiar slippery smell of oil, agitated his nostrils. He almost sneezed.

"You're pale," Artkin taunted.

Which Miro expected. Artkin had always taunted

him, and Miro had learned to absorb the taunts without comment. Perhaps he would not have been able to answer, anyway. His throat was tight, constricted. He was afraid that if he tried to talk he would not be able to gather enough saliva and would somehow choke.

"You'll be all right," Artkin assured him, his voice suddenly kind. That was Artkin—abrasive one moment, gentle the next. He had also killed three people in Miro's presence in the past two years, each of them in cold blood. And now it was Miro's turn to follow Artkin's example.

Artkin smiled. But now contempt edged the smile. "After all, you are sixteen."

Miro tried not to show his anger. He tightened his lips, kept his cheeks taut. He was furious that Artkin should think that killing someone—who? a bus driver? a nothing?—should bother him. Or perhaps Artkin was taunting him again to keep him keen, on edge, sharp. Either way, Miro was angry. He was not a child anymore. And inflicting death did not bother him. Neither did the contemplation of the act. He had been waiting for four, almost five years now. How else could he justify his existence, make his life meaningful before it was taken from him? His brother, Aniel, had died too soon, before making his mark, before fulfilling his promise. No, Miro was not apprehensive about the delivery of death; he worried only that he would not do a professional job.

"Let us review the plan," Artkin said, formal and precise, but the sneer always close to his lips. Like Elvis Presley when he sang certain songs. Miro allowed his eyelids to half close now, not really listening to Artkin rehearse the plan yet again. Miro had learned the trick of humming silently, running a song through his mind, and he did this now, an old Presley song without the sneer in it, "Love Me Tender," not like some of Presley's more raucous songs. Artkin did not like distractions, particularly when he was outlining plans. He liked to review plans the way other people like to play cards. And he did not approve of foolishness like Miro's fondness for Presley's music or other American diversions: those television cartoons, for instance, that Miro lost himself in every Saturday morning if a television set was at hand. Miro continued to hum soundlessly as he listened to Artkin review the plan. Overtaking the bus, driving to the bridge, killing the driver, waiting for the first message to be delivered. Suddenly, Miro thought: What is the driver doing this minute? Did he have any premonition of his death? Did he know that tomorrow at this time he would be mute, silent, still forever?

Silence fell in the small room as Artkin completed his recitation. Miro looked out at the sleepy street below. Main Street. Hallowell, Massachusetts. United States of America. So far from his homeland. But we have no homeland, Artkin always said, and this was true. Still, Miro was gripped by a clutch of lonesomeness that was so intense his stomach lurched and he turned from the window. He wished this small cramped room that smelled of urine and grease and gun oil contained at least a television set. For diversion at moments like this, sudden moments when homesickness came without warning.

"We are forever homesick," Artkin had once said in a rare moment of tenderness, "because our land does not exist anymore, gobbled up and occupied by others."

"What is your name?"
"Miro."

"No, your real name."

"Miro Shantas."

"No, not this name, not this fake name you have taken. But your real one."

"I have not taken a fake name. My name is Miro Shantas."

"Look, this is not an exercise. I am not testing you. I wish for you to say your real name."

Miro slitted his eyes, studying Artkin, trying to determine if Artkin were really serious about his name or whether he was playing some kind of game. He had to admit that Artkin's face was dark and intense, his eyes brooding; there was nothing playful in his attitude. Miro looked away, toward the jukebox where someone was studying the selections. The restaurant was small; barely a restaurant, more like a quick-lunch diner, a place for truck drivers, transients. Like us, Artkin said. We never stay, and where we linger even for a moment, we must never rest or let down.

Miro's coffee was cold as he sipped it. He wished the fellow at the jukebox would slip in the coin and start the music. Something by the Bee Gees, maybe. Or Elvis.

"So," Artkin said, patient, waiting, the most patient man in the world. "Tell me your real name."

Miro decided to make his own test, play his own game, for once.

"But you know my real name," Miro said.

"If I knew it, would I ask you to say it?" Artkin said.

"Yes," Miro said.

"And why would I ask you something that I already know?"

"Because you are Artkin and anything is possible with you."

Artkin did not really smile, but the angles of his face

altered. Something danced in his eyes, not anything resembling laughter but a lightness. He wondered how old Artkin was. Thirty? Forty? It was impossible to tell. Sometimes in the early morning, before dawn, waiting in a car somewhere—like that time in Philadelphia when they could not return to the room because of the police—Artkin's flesh would look pale and gray, his eyes like burned-out lamps. He would look one hundred years old, a thousand. Other times, outlining one of his plans or waiting for that moment when action would begin, he seemed youthful, ageless, eyes lit up by an inner source. But these moments came and went swiftly. Most of the time, he was Artkin: emotionless, a machine capable of sudden startling deeds. Now, the light still danced in his eyes, and Miro realized that Artkin was enjoying himself. A rare moment.

"If you know me so well, then you must know that when I ask your real name, I expect you to tell me," Artkin said. His hands were on the table—and what remained of his fingers. The middle fingers of his left hand were stubs of varying lengths, the result of a bomb that had detonated too soon. "It's good you are right-handed," Miro had said once, watching Artkin deftly manipulating a knife with his right hand. Artkin had replied: "I was left-handed."

My real name, Miro thought now. He had not thought of his real name for such a long time that he had to dig back into his memory for it. Do not simply forget your name but bury it, the instructor had said. Bury it so that it never betrays you. Choose a name that is unlike your own or even the place of your origin. You must carry nothing with you that may betray you and that includes your name most of all.

Miro wondered: What is Artkin's real name?

The waitress approached, a thin girl of eighteen or so with a terrible complexion, her face like the surface of the moon.

"Anything else?" she asked, pencil poised to total their check.

"That will be all, Myra," Artkin said.

"What did you say?" she asked.

"I said, 'That will be all, Myra.' "

"My name's not Myra," the girl said.

Artkin smiled at her. "Of course it isn't," he said. But his voice suggested the opposite, his voice and his smile. They hinted wickedly of deep secrets.

"Well, it isn't," she said. "My name's Bonnie. And not a nickname either. I was baptized Bonnie although the priest didn't like it because there's no Saint Bonnie."

"Please give us the check, Myra," Artkin said, voice cold now, uninterested.

"I said my name's not Myra," she muttered as she totaled up the bill.

"Myra's a nice name. It's nothing to be ashamed of," Artkin said.

Her face reddened, accentuating the acne, the pimples and small scabs. Artkin could do that to people, intimidate them, draw them into conversations they did not want to be drawn into, force them into confrontations.

"Think about it, Myra. How old were you when you were baptized? Two weeks, two months? Do you remember being baptized with the name Bonnie? Of course not. It's what people have told you. Have you ever seen your birth certificate? Not the thing they give you when you go to City Hall for a copy, but the original? The one that says your name is Myra. You've never seen it, have you? But that doesn't mean it does not exist. You have never seen me before but I exist. I have existed all this time. I might have been there when you were baptized. Myra."

She stood there for a moment, the check in her hand, hesitant, doubtful, her eyes wary, and Miro knew that this was what Artkin had worked to do: create this split second of doubt and hesitation. He knew that he had reached his mark, drawn blood. Then the moment vanished. The girl flung the check on the table.

"You're nuts," she said, and turned away, shaking her head at all the strange people loose in the world.

Artkin looked at Miro. He smiled. As much of a smile as he ever allowed himself.

Miro leaned across the table toward him and almost upset his cup and saucer.

"My name," he said, slowly and distinctly, "is Miro. Miro Shantas. My real and only name."

Music burst from the jukebox, a song Miro didn't recognize but it was loud and upbeat, disco, the kind of music Artkin despised.

Again Artkin's face altered, and this time there was almost admiration in his eyes. "I salute you, Miro Shantas," he said.

Artkin seldom gave praise. Miro felt a flush of warmth as he basked in that praise, content suddenly. He let himself be carried by the music.

The next morning, they waited in the brown and beige van at the intersection of Water Street and Vinton Avenue. The bus was late, but this did not disturb Artkin or Miro or the others. Artkin had studied the situation for weeks. He knew the bus schedule was erratic, depending on how long the bus had to wait at the home of each child. There was no central gathering point for the children; they were picked up individually at their homes. Some streaked out to the bus, others dallied. They were young: all under six, babies, really. The bus took them to a day camp near a placid pond in Hallowell, where they frolicked and swam and did all the things children did, until late in the afternoon. There were sixteen children. Artkin said he was prepared to kill at least two of them. Perhaps more, depending.

Miro stood at the back of the van, watching the morning activity on Water Street. There was not much activity. A boy rode by on a bicycle trying to balance a fishing line across the handlebars. A dog sniffed at some bushes and then lifted his leg and urinated. Miro did not know what kind of dog or what kind of bushes. He watched the dog go off. He considered all the things he did not know, how his schooling had been intense and narrow, with no diversions, no time to identify flowers and bushes. Besides, the bushes and trees and other growths in his homeland—ah, but he had no homeland—were different. Just as the people were different. And the food. In the matter of food, Miro felt himself a traitor; he was enchanted by American food, hamburgers and hot dogs and potato chips. He watched the television commercials for McDonald's and Burger King and others with pleasure. He told no one about these small pleasures. Anyway, who was there to tell?

Miro glanced at his watch: almost nine. They were waiting for the orange bus to pull up and then for a blond, plump child to dash from the house to the bus. The last child. Miro was impatient. He wanted to act. He thought how long he had waited for this moment, the long rehearsal that had been his entire life about to be over.

Artkin said: "They are always late. With children, you must play it loose and be patient."

No one commented. Artkin was in the passenger seat;

actually there were no seats, they had been removed to provide room for the four of them plus the equipment. Stroll, the black, was in the driver's position, hands loose on the steering wheel. He drove a car or any vehicle as if he were conducting a symphony. Miro had seen him careen through the streets of Brooklyn after the post office explosion as if he were on holiday, without a care in the world. He was usually silent and sullen and came alive only when there was driving to be done. The other man was Antibbe, heavy, middle-aged, at least forty. His grimace could be like thunder rumbling, his frown an earthquake. He lumbered through life like a freight car on the loose, shouldering his way through exits and entrances. He seldom spoke and when he did, his words came out in hoarse grunts.

Miro felt for the warmth of the weapon against his chest, inside the jacket. The morning was hot: late August, although Miro was frequently confused about the seasons; too many of them in one brief year, not like his homeland. Looking out the rear window, he saw a young girl walking on the sidewalk, her arms swinging at her sides, black hair sparkling, her full white blouse bright in the sun. American girls: he could not become accustomed to their blunt sexuality, the clinging jeans, the tight sweaters, the frankness of their faces holding few secrets. In his homeland, sexuality was implied, hinted at, not exactly concealed but delicately veiled. He had been in the United States for almost three years and was still both fascinated and repelled by so much of what he saw. So much that was brazen, hectic, loud, raw, and coarse. But then suddenly tender. Like Presley's music. He wished Artkin allowed him to take his transistor on operations.

Miro watched the girl coming nearer, nearer, involved in her own affairs, late for works perhaps, her blouse moving pleasantly in the sunshine, not knowing the effect her body had on people. A year ago, Artkin, noticing Miro's discomfort in the presence of females, said: "I will obtain one for you." Miro had replied angrily: "Don't bother." He did not want Artkin or anyone procuring a female for him. He was not like those people who gathered in theaters where girls and women danced without clothes. He hated Times Square in New York City, where everything was cheap and loud. He could wait. But, wait for what? The law of averages would settle the question; he knew that he would be dead before he reached twenty or twenty-one. His brother had died at seventeen, in the Detroit confrontation.

The girl passed by, went out of his sight, and Miro resisted touching himself. He turned red-faced from the window and touched his gun in consolation.

"The bus comes," Artkin said.

Miro heard the slow screech of brakes as the bus stopped farther up the street. He craned his neck to look through the windshield and saw the orange vehicle a hundred yards away. He glanced at his watch. They would overtake the bus in seven minutes on a deserted stretch of road outside the town. In another twenty minutes, they would be at the bridge. Fifteen and seven were twenty-two. Allow three minutes for unexpected events. (Always allow, Artkin said repeatedly.) So, within twenty-five minutes, I will have killed my first man. A man will have died because of me.

But it turned out not to be a man.

When they boarded the bus, the driver sitting behind the wheel was a girl. Blond, slender, wearing a dazzling yellow jersey. Long hair like straw; no, not straw, honey, syrup.

Miro had followed Artkin to the bus after Stroll had overtaken the vehicle, pulled the van up in front of it, and forced the driver to come to a halt. Artkin, Antibbe, and Miro had scrambled out of the van while Stroll remained at the wheel. Antibbe easily forced the door open with a crowbar and returned to the van. Artkin and Miro had climbed aboard. The takeover was completed within seconds, with no outcry from the children or the girl driver. She regarded them in shocked silence, mouth agape, eyes wide with disbelief. Miro crouched down beside her to remain out of sight of anyone passing on the highway while Artkin passed down the aisle, greeting the children, calling to them— *Hello, there. . . . It's a nice day. . . . Aren't you a pretty little girl? . . . Do you like candy, chocolate?*—all the while watching for any passing vehicles. He cajoled the children, diverted them, a master of that kind of thing, a superb actor. Miro envied him as he remained beside the girl. For the first time she noticed the gun in Miro's hand. Her face registered revulsion, as if she had observed something obscene. And then fright overcame her: stronger than fright. Terror. She had run the course Miro had so often seen. Shock then revulsion then terror.

Artkin returned to the front of the bus and picked up a brown grocery bag he had dropped on entering. The bag contained chocolate candy, wrapped in tinfoil.

"Candy for everybody—everybody loves candy," he called out brightly. Miro touched Artkin's arm. Artkin paused. Miro saw the pulse leap in Artkin's throat; it was dangerous to touch Artkin.

Miro raised himself up. "I thought you said the driver was a man." His voice was a whisper but harsher than he intended.

"You are not supposed to think," Artkin said, spitting

the words, pulling away, going down the aisle, distributing the candy among eager hands. The candy had been treated with a tranquilizer, a drug strong enough to render the children docile and passive within a few minutes. How else, Artkin had said, can we keep a bus full of children quiet? There was plenty of chocolate, as well as lollipops dipped in the drug in spare bags in the van.

Miro crouched beside the girl again. Her knuckles were white where they clutched the steering wheel. She was rigid, looking ahead through the windshield. Her chin trembled and her shoulders shook as if a chill had overtaken her. Miro remembered that one time when his own chin had trembled and his shoulders had shuddered beyond control. When Aniel died. He had fought tears—a soldier was not supposed to cry—but he had been overwhelmed at how the rest of his body betrayed him although his eyes had remained dry. He had tried to remain emotionless, to keep the fact of Aniel's death neutral and meaningless, but a strange sound had issued from his body, a sob torn from his insides, as if giving voice to a terrible wound. Artkin, who was always there, dug a hard hand into Miro's shoulders. He had brought the news of Aniel's death: instantaneous, almost accidental—a bullet had ricocheted and drilled into Aniel's forehead, between his eyes. Miro had wrenched himself away from Artkin's grip and bolted from the room, disgusted and in despair, disgusted with the way his body had betrayed him after all those years of training and in despair because his brother's death left him alone in the world. Except for Artkin. But Artkin was not his flesh and blood.

Miro studied the girl now. He was close enough to smell the scent of her deodorant. Or was it her cologne?

She raised her arm slightly and he saw the circle of perspiration at her armpit. So, the girl's body was betraying her just as Miro's body had once betrayed him. As all bodies must eventually become traitors, perhaps. And Artkin? Would he ever become a victim of his own betrayal?

Miro looked at the girl's temple near that flow of yellow hair. The plan had been for him to walk the driver outside the bus, away from the sight of the children, raise the pistol to the driver's temple, and squeeze gently, carefully. Do it quickly, Artkin had advised, and do not hesitate. Artkin had often said they were not interested in needless cruelty. They had a job to do and the job concerned death. Do not prolong it more than necessary. Deliver it as efficiently as possible with the least mess. We are not animals, after all, he said, but merely a means to an end. Everything is done for a purpose. Miro reached out his hand as if to touch the girl's temple or perhaps her hair. But he resisted the impulse.

Artkin had finished handing out the candy and now he laughed and joked with the children, although Miro knew his eyes contained no laughter. The tranquilizers should have begun to take effect by the time they reached the bridge. Miro wondered whether the revolver's report would rouse them again.

As Artkin returned to the front of the bus, the girl drew a deep breath and turned to them. "What's this all about?" she demanded, gathering her strength and courage and outrage, not realizing how pathetic she sounded.

"Just drive, miss," Artkin said, softly, gently. "Don't be concerned. We merely want to divert the bus from its course for a few minutes. No harm will be done to you or the children."

Miro marveled at how convincing Artkin sounded. He had seen him do this before, his voice reassuring, soothing, almost tender. He remembered that voice vividly just before Artkin had shattered the face of the police officer in Detroit with a blast from the revolver. If the thousand pieces of that face were put back together now, the countenance just before death would be peaceful, expectant, without any hint of the horror to come.

"Why are you driving this bus today?" Miro asked. He knew this question would draw Artkin's wrath—Artkin always discouraged needless conversation in operations—but Miro was disturbed. He did not want anything to go wrong with his first death.

"My uncle is sick. I take over sometimes for him. I passed a special driver education course." Like a schoolgirl reciting her lesson.

Artkin darted Miro a glance of annoyance and then turned to the girl. "I'm certain you are a careful driver, miss, and that's good. We would not want anything to happen to the children. Just keep driving so the children do not become upset." His voice still reassuring, reasonable.

The girl actually smiled at Artkin, a wan smile, uncertain perhaps, but a smile all the same.

Artkin looked at his watch. Miro glanced at the kids in the bus. Some of them seemed to have gone limp and sat languidly in the seats, as if in a daze. Miro wondered: How strong were those drugs?

"You have seventeen minutes left," Artkin said to him.

Miro nodded. For a moment, he had been as deceived by Artkin's gentleness as the girl had been. But the reality of the situation imposed itself again on him. He glanced at his watch. In seventeen minutes—no, sixteen now—he would kill this girl. He wondered how old she was. Eighteen? Seventeen? His own age?

The girl shifted gears as the van in front of them began an uphill climb. The children barely stirred. Miro saw Artkin pondering the children. He looked doubtful, his forehead wrinkled in concern. Artkin seldom showed doubt. Had the drugs been too powerful? Or was Artkin merely deep in thought, selecting his possible victims: who would die, who would live?

Artkin became conscious of Miro's study.

"Don't concern yourself with them," he said, indicating the children. "Look to her." He nodded toward the girl. "You have less than fifteen minutes."

Miro felt the presence of the gun under his jacket, like a tumor growing there.

She was furious with herself. Her pants were wet—her panties, really, but she hated the word *panties* for some reason—and her fingers actually ached where she gripped the steering wheel and she could feel a migraine beginning, a dart of pain imbedded in her forehead above her right eyebrow, but these things didn't matter. What mattered most—what she was furious about—was the way she had sat there all the time, numb and dumb, while these animals took over the bus, took complete control of her and the children while she did absolutely nothing at all. And those wet pants, her flesh chilled now between her legs. Her bladder and the muscles there—always a weakness. A sneeze could do it, or sudden laughter, and she would feel a small oozing of delight followed by the shameful knowledge that she was wet again. She owned sixteen pairs of pants—all right, panties—but, jeez, this was the limit.

She kept her eyes on the van ahead, following orders. Ordinarily, she hated to follow orders—at home or at school—but usually did. Another weakness. And here she was, complying again, carrying out the instructions they had given her. Not they: him. The older one. The one in command. Funny, you'd think she'd be more intimidated by the older one rather than the boy, but it was the boy who worried her. Even now, she could feel his intensity as he crouched nearby. Even though he had put the gun away, in his jacket someplace, she felt a sense of dread, menace. He had looked at her with those deep brown eyes, almost black, and she felt as though he were measuring her for a coffin. God, what a thought. But then she always dramatized situations. Anyway, the boy disturbed her, not the man. The man had seemed reasonable, rational, unlike the boy, who had something of an animal about him, like a dog straining at a leash.

The van took a sudden turn to the left. Old Vineyard Road. She was puzzled—there was nothing out that way. She had lived in Hallowell all her life and knew the place like she knew her own face in the mirror—even the small pimple that appeared near her nose each time her period arrived—and she tried to envision where the van was leading her and the bus. To Brook's End? That old pavilion where they'd had dances years ago during the Big Band era her parents always talked about? Nothing else out there. Anything could happen out there in the woods like that. She gripped the wheel hard to keep from trembling. Stop dramatizing, she told herself again. Think of the poor kids. She glanced in the rear-view mirror. The kids were subdued, not restless or jabbering as usual. She saw one child apparently dozing, her chin resting on her thin chest. Another child's mouth hung open, his jaw slack and loose. She knew instantly that the children had been drugged, that the candy the older man had given out was evidently doped up. As she darted glances from the van ahead to the rear-view mirror, she saw a boy begin to fall lazily, almost in slow motion, out of his seat, into the aisle. She cried out. The older man had also seen the child begin to fall and hurried to him, catching him before he hit the floor. He picked up the little boy, cradling him in his arms. Instead of restoring the child to the seat, the man himself sat down, holding the boy against his own chest, rubbing his hand across the boy's forehead paternally. Yet the man was obviously a monster, taking over a bus like this, feeding the kids some kind of drug.

"Keep your eyes on the road," the boy told her. His words were precise, each word pronounced perfectly. Too perfectly. He had a slight accent, an echo of something ancient in his voice, and it was obvious that English was not his native language. She glanced at him quickly, defiantly, to show that she would not always leap to obey his orders. His hair was black, small tight curls fitting his head like a helmet. His skin was dark but with a kind of copper hue as if burned by the sun too long. He could be anything. From anywhere.

Now she had to concentrate on the driving because the road was unpaved, rough and narrow. Trees formed arches through which the vehicles passed. The sunshine was blotted out occasionally and they were enveloped in sudden shadows. The bus lurched as it encountered a dip in the road, and the boy was thrown slightly against her. She felt his body against her shoulder only for a moment, but it caused her to shudder. She looked into the mirror. The small pimple had appeared, near her right nostril. Damn it. She hadn't noticed the pimple this morning when she washed her face, and her period was two weeks away. The migraine ate like acid into her forehead. Would her period come ahead of time while she was here on the bus? She felt like crying, the way she had when she was a little girl and crying solved things, brought rescue.

"Where are we going?" she asked, fleeing her thoughts.

"Just continue to drive," the boy said. "We are almost there."

She sent her mind ahead of the bus and the van, pondering the possible destination. At the same time, the van began a steep climb and she felt the resistance of the bus to the ascent. She shifted into second, summoning all her strength for the movement. This was an old bus, without automatic shifting, and the gear mechanism balked at changes, the gears grinding in protest, like old bones being disturbed.

Her mind flashed ahead again. At the top of the hill the road continued its twisting way in the woods. The road crossed a railroad track no longer in use. She remembered that there was an old rickety railroad bridge off to the right, abandoned, closed off. The trains from Boston did not come this far anymore. Freight trains took other routes and commuter trains from Boston took passengers only as far as Concord and Lexington, twenty miles away. The old bridge was a narrow sagging span high above the Moosock River, which was no longer a river but a thin scrawl of water, barely a brook. Kids sometimes invaded the bridge and removed the traffic barrier—a gate as old and battered as the bridge itself. They held beer parties and dropped the bottles to the river below. She hadn't participated in the parties, but their fame was legendary at Hallowell High.

The bus climbed steadily, lumbering, like some huge beast being driven against its will. She hoped the bus would collapse, like a beast, and die there on the road. She wondered what would happen if the bus stopped and didn't go on. She looked down at the ignition. What would happen if she removed the key, tossed it out the window into the thick growth by the side of the road? Would this spoil their plan, whatever it was? Or would she be placing the kids and herself in worse jeopardy? The man seemed reasonable. Should she go along with him and hope that what he said about diverting the bus for only a few moments was the truth? She looked into the rear-view mirror again. The children were lolling in their seats, some asleep, others half awake, eyelids drooping. They're my responsibility, she told herself. They're in my care. I shouldn't do anything to place them in greater danger than they're already in. She felt the presence of the boy beside her, smelled the plastic jacket he wore. He was groping inside the jacket now: reaching for the gun? The migraine was a dagger above her right eye.

"We are almost there," the boy said.

And the gun was in his hand again. Pointing at her.

The van had halted in front of the bus at the top of the hill.

The man, having dispatched the boy to watch the children, said, "The van will reverse itself and back onto the bridge. You will follow."

"Do I back up, too?" she asked, wondering how she could perform such a stunt on this narrow dirt road.

"No, simply follow the van. It will stop and you will stop, too, facing it."

"It's a railroad bridge," she said. "And it's old and rickety. Is it strong enough to hold us?"

"Yes. It has been tested recently. It is not too narrow, as you will see. There's room for two sets of tracks. But proceed slowly. The ride may be uncomfortable as the tires must go over the railroad ties. The bridge is perhaps three hundred feet long, the length of one of your football fields." She noted the use of *your*—meaning not mine. She wondered about his nationality. He was dark like the boy and his skin was also coppery, burned by the sun too long.

The driver of the van had somehow turned it around, although he left broken bushes behind.

"Now follow," the man said. "And then it will be all over for you."

"Will I be free to go? The children—what about them?"

He touched her shoulder gently. "Don't be concerned. Everything will be fine."

She followed the van onto the bridge. The ride was bumpy, the bus bouncing as the wheels passed over the wooden railroad ties. She suddenly had an impression of height and realized that the bridge was high, probably one hundred and fifty feet or so above the river. The sensation of height was emphasized by the spaces between the railroad ties. Leaning forward and craning her neck, she saw clear space every few feet. Anyone walking on the bridge would have to watch his step. She urged the bus forward delicately, conscious of the spindly structure, the rotting ties, the space yawning below. The guardrails were solid-looking, however; black, iron, providing a sense of safety. Her foot barely touched the accelerator as she guided the bus in the bouncing path of the van ahead.

"Fine," the man said, "fine."

At last, the van halted and she braked the bus. She looked across the ravine to the old pavilion building. The building, abandoned, lopsided as if frozen in a drunken sway, was perched on the edge of land that was as high as the bridge. It seemed far away, the length of three or four football fields.

"Turn off the motor," the man said.

When she complied, the man reached over and took the key out of the ignition. He slipped it into his jacket pocket. "You did excellently," he said. Then he turned away. "Miro," he called.

But Miro didn't answer. In fact, he heard Artkin's voice as if from a great distance. He was looking at one of the children, a boy. The boy was alone in a seat, not paired off like most of the others. He lay full-length across the seat, as if he were sleeping. But his skin was bluish, as if someone had injected the veins of his face with blue dye. His chest did not rise or fall.

"Artkin," Miro cried, unable to take his eyes away from the child.

"Yes?" Artkin replied, voice sharp, impatient.

Miro managed to tear his eyes away from the boy. He beckoned to Artkin. A flash of annoyance crossed Artkin's face as he walked down the aisle toward Miro. "It's your time," he said, as he approached. Miro pointed at the boy.

Artkin swore, in the old language, swore softly, an ancient word of dismay and disgust. Miro had never heard such a word from Artkin's lips before. Then Artkin acted quickly, feeling the boy's chest for signs of life, checking the pulse in the frail wrist, placing his ear against the boy's lips. The boy was still, unmoving.

"Is something the matter?" the girl called, her voice anxious. "Is one of the children sick?"

"Check the other children," Artkin told the boy. "See if they are all right." To the girl, he called: "One moment, miss."

Miro made a quick tour of the children. Some were half awake, reposing in partial slumber. Others slept, their faces slack with sleep, bodies limp and loose. But they all seemed normal. All seemed to be breathing regularly. He reported his findings to Artkin, who was working on the boy, massaging his chest, breathing into his mouth.

Miro looked toward the girl. She had turned in her seat and was regarding Miro and Artkin with apprehension. Miro felt his anger rising. If this had not happened with the child, he would now be carrying out his assignment. First, the girl had appeared as the driver instead of the man as planned. And now this delay. He felt his stomach muscles tightening. Looking at the dead child once more, he pondered how quickly death could arrive. He looked away from the child, that blue flesh, the body so still. Why should this death concern him? He had seen death more violently, more sickening. He remembered the man in the Detroit operation who had soiled his trousers the moment before he died, the stench filling the car. But this child seemed so defenseless, and his death was without purpose. Artkin had planned the death of some children if it became necessary, when the greatest effect could be obtained. Another thing: Artkin did not like unexpected happenings, unplanned developments. One of the most important parts of an operation, he said, was anticipation. So that there would be no surprises, or at least a minimum, and minor ones, at that.

"Miro," Artkin said, "come closer."

The girl called again: "What's going on? Is somebody sick?"

"One moment, please," Artkin told the girl. And then to Miro, although he wasn't looking at Miro. He was looking at the dead child and when he spoke, it was in a whisper. "The child is dead, Miro, and we have to take that death into account. But we can turn this to our advantage. In fact, this may be more effective than the girl's death. It will shock them, the death of a child, but it will also show them that we are not bluffing, that we are adamant."

He stood up and faced Miro. "We must improvise, Miro. For the moment, we do nothing about the girl except watch her carefully. I am afraid of the drugs. They are very powerful, as you can see, more powerful that I had thought they would be. I do not wish to drug them further at this time. We do not want a bus full of dead children—that would destroy the plan, everything. They are our bargaining power. So, we wait. The girl can help us to take care of them, keep them quiet."

"But—" Miro began to protest. His first major assignment, his initiation into the brotherhood, and now it was being set aside. He had prepared himself for this moment, girded his loins, waited for years; and now it was postponed, delayed, canceled perhaps.

"You will have your chance, Miro," Artkin said kindly. "When we see that no other children are affected by the drug, we will give them more. This boy was perhaps allergic. Or had a weak heart. An exception." He looked toward the girl, who continued to gaze at them with concern on her face. "The girl must die, Miro. She has seen us without the masks and she must die. And you will see that she does. But not yet, not just yet. Be patient. She is more useful to us alive, for the moment."

Miro acquiesced, saw the reasonableness of the move. He knew what Artkin had long ago taught him: The plan was of first importance, of only importance, all else paled beside the plan. Their actions were meaningless, worth nothing, in fact were abominations without the plan.

"Go to the girl now. Tell her what happened. Explain that it was an accident. Find out her name, everything you can about her. Win her confidence. I will be busy with other things."

Miro nodded, starting away.

"And put on your mask, Miro. It is time. By now, the messages have been sent and we can expect action at any moment."

The mask.

Miro both loved and hated the mask. Actually, it was not a mask but a modified version of a hood worn by skiers. The material was some kind of fabric with an inside lining of man-made material the Americans were clever at producing. The lining kept the skin cool while somehow absorbing the perspiration. The mask dangled from a button inside Miro's jacket. The jacket was the one he always wore on assignments. Dark brown, hidden pockets, two sizes too large, to allow extra equipment to be carried easily—the Swiss army knife, the pliers, the screwdriver set. Plus the holster for the gun.

Miro reached for the mask but decided to talk to the girl before putting it on. He would be able to communicate with her more easily that way. Sometimes, in fact, he felt like a prisoner in the mask, as if he were locked inside, looking out at the world but not part of it. The mask did not cover his eyes, of course, or his nostrils or mouth. There were two small openings, barely notice-able, at the ears: weblike fabric covered the ears so that his hearing would not be impaired. But he did not always feel comfortable in the mask.

And yet there were things he loved about the mask. Looking at himself in the mirror the first time he put it on, when he was thirteen or so, he realized that his age was disguised. He could have been twenty-three or thirty-three, a boy no longer. Men's faces paled when they confronted him in the mask, men many years older and much bigger and stronger. The mask gave him a sense of power and authority.

Sometimes, however, he brooded about the mask. He had the feeling that he must be doing something dishonorable if the operations and confrontations had to be carried out with faces hidden. If what we are doing is heroic, to deliver our people and restore our home-land, why must we hide who we are? he once asked Artkin. And Artkin had told him that there were many laws in the world, good laws and bad laws, right laws and wrong laws. According to the wrong laws, their mission, their work, was condemned. But these laws had been made by their enemies. So they had to disguise themselves to remain free under the wrong laws.

Miro held the mask in his hand now. It was black with red stitching around the eyes, nostrils, and mouth. The moment when he first put it on in an operation was always exhilarating; it was the gesture that divided his life. Without the mask, he was Miro Shantas, the boy without even a real name to identify him to the world. With the mask, he was Miro Shantas, freedom fighter. He often wondered which person he really was.

Okay. She wasn't panicky. She listened to the boy, telling herself to be sharp, alert, on her toes, cheerleading herself onward. She knew the boy's name was Miro and the man was Artkin. She'd heard them exchanging names a few moments ago, and somehow the realization that they had names restored a sense of normality to the situation, reduced the degree of terror that had engulfed her during the bus ride to the bridge. *Miro, Artkin* was much better than *the boy, the man,* rendering them human. And yet what this boy named Miro was telling her now was inhuman, a horror story. The child was dead.

"Murdered," she said, the word leaping to her lips, an alien word she had never uttered before in its real meaning.

"Not murder, miss," the boy said. "It was an accident. We were told the drugs were safe, but this boy died."

"Does this mean the other kids are in danger, too?"

"No. We have checked them all—you can see for yourself—and they are normal. Perhaps this boy had a weak heart. Or he was allergic to the drugs." He pronounced "allergic" as three separate words.

Kate turned to look at the children. They were still subdued, although some yawned and stirred restlessly in their seats.

"We want you to help us with the children," the boy said. "Take care of them. See to their needs. This will convince you that we mean them no harm."

"How long are we going to be here?" she asked. She nodded toward the man, who was going from seat to seat, touching the children, their foreheads, their cheeks, speaking to them gently and soothingly. "He said it would be all over when we reached the bridge."

Miro thought fast. "We have had a change of plans. Because of the death of the boy. We will be here a bit longer."

"How long?" she asked, pressing on, sensing a sudden uncertainty in the boy.

He shrugged. "No one knows, really. A few hours . . ."

At that moment, a noise at the door claimed her attention. The big lumbering man who had forced open the door with a crowbar was back at the door again. He shattered the windows in the door with a rock.

"What's he doing?" she asked.

The man broke the glass with a glowering intensity, looking neither at the girl nor at Miro.

"He is breaking the glass to put a lock on the door so that it cannot be opened with the handle there," Miro said.

Her glance went automatically to the emergency door on the left halfway down the bus. The boy did not miss the direction her eyes had taken. He did not smile; he seemed incapable of smiling. But his eyes brightened. "The emergency door will be locked with a clamp," he said. "And the windows—we will seal the windows shut. It is useless to think of escaping."

She felt mildly claustrophobic and also transparent, as if the boy could see right into her mind. Turning away, she saw the man standing now at the seat where the dead boy lay. She wondered which child was dead and yet, in a way, she didn't want to know. An anonymous death didn't seem so terrible. She didn't really know any of the children, anyway, although their faces were familiar from the few times she'd substituted for her uncle. She'd heard them call each other by name— Tommy, Karen, Monique. But she couldn't place names with faces.

"May I see the child?" she asked. And realized she didn't really want to see the child. Not a dead child. But she felt it was her responsibility to see him, to corroborate the fact of his death.

Miro paused.

"What is your name?" he asked.

"Kate. Kate Forrester."

"My name is Miro," he said. He realized that this was perhaps the first time he had ever introduced himself to anyone. Usually, he was anonymous. Or Artkin would say "The boy's name is Miro" when they encountered strangers.

Kate pretended that she hadn't learned his name earlier. "And your friend's name?" she asked.

"Artkin," he said.

The huge man outside the bus was now testing the lock. Kate didn't care to know *his* name. His name would only establish his existence in her life, and he was so ugly and menacing that she didn't want to acknowledge him at all. She glanced at the van and saw the black fellow at the wheel, staring into space, as if in a dream world of his own, not really here in the van, on the bridge.

"Please," Kate said. "May I see the child?"

Miro shrugged. "We are going to be together for a while on this bus. You should call me Miro and I should call you Kate." Miro found the words difficult to say, particularly to a girl and an American girl at that. But Artkin had told him to win her confidence.

The girl didn't answer. Miro, flustered, turned away and then beckoned her to follow him. He led her to the center of the bus. "She wants to see him," he told Artkin.

Kate drew a deep breath and looked down. The child lay still, as if asleep. His pallor had a bluish tint. Miro also looked, seeing the child from the girl's viewpoint, wondering what she thought. Had she ever seen a dead person before? Probably not; not in her well-scrubbed American world. The girl shuddered slightly. "Come," Miro said. She looked grateful as she turned away from the child. At least she had not fainted. Her flesh was pale, however, and this somehow made her blond hair more pronounced, more radiant. He realized that American boys would consider her beautiful.

Artkin accompanied them to the front of the bus.

"What happens now?" Kate asked. Would she ever forget that blue child on the bus seat?

"As far as your part is concerned, miss," Artkin said, "it will consist mostly of waiting. For a few hours. We have sent messages and are waiting for a reply. Meanwhile, you will care for the children. They will be awakening soon. I want you to reassure them. Most of all, keep them in control, keep them quiet."

Kate closed her eyes. The migraine reasserted itself, digging into her forehead. The blue face of the dead child floated in the darkness. She realized she didn't even known his name. Escaping from that face, she opened her eyes to confront the two strangers before her. The full import of what was going on suddenly rushed into full and terrible comprehension.

"I know what you are," she said. She did not recognize her voice: it was strident, off key, too loud in her ears, the voice of a stranger. "You're holding us hostage and you've made demands. You're going to hold us here until the demands are met. You're—" She faltered, unable to say the word. Hijackers. Her mind was crowded with newspaper headlines and television newscasts of hijackings all over the world, gunfire and explosions, innocent persons killed, even children.

"This is no concern of yours," Artkin said, his voice cold, the words snapping like whips. "The children are your concern. Nothing else. See to the children."

She drew back as if he had struck her.

Turning to Miro, Artkin said: "It is time for the masks."

She saw them take the masks out of their jackets. They pulled them over their heads. They had suddenly become grotesque, monstrous, figures escaped from her worst nightmares. And she saw her own doom in the masks.

She wet her pants so badly that the trickles down her thighs were like the caresses of moist and obscene fingers.

part
3

Another picture postcard from the collected works of Benjamin Marchand: Nettie Halversham.

Color the postcard to do justice to Nettie Halversham's beauty: eyes the color of bruises, hair like the shining black of old classic automobiles, lips like crushed strawberries. Ridiculous? Maybe. But, God, Nettie Halversham was—is—beautiful. And her heart was also black like the color of those classic cars.

Edge the postcard with guilt because guilt whistles through the tunnel in my chest. Guilt of all shades and colors plus the guilt that sends me to Brimmler's Bridge when I should be directing snowballs at Martingale and

Donateli or contemplating the amber brew in the township of Pompey.

The guilt, however, really starts with Nettie Halversham.

Because.

Because, all during the time of the seizure of the bus, when those kids were being held as hostages and the television stations were giving out all kinds of bulletins, and Fort Delta was in a state of emergency—a bodyguard was even assigned to me and Jackie Brenner and other kids whose fathers were in positions of authority at Delta—anyway, during all that time, the headlines and the sirens screaming, I could think only of myself and how miserable I was, and I'd sit and stare at the telephone for hours. Or what seemed like hours. Once, I put my hand on the phone to pick it up and the guard came alert and said: "Who are you calling?"

He was a big guy. He looked like a former football player, or maybe a boxer. His ears were smashed and his nose was twisted. He was the original on which the cliché was based. He made me nervous because he just didn't guard the house and all; he stayed with me, in the same room, every minute. He'd watch me when I ate, and he never wanted anything to eat himself. I figured if he ate with me I wouldn't feel so self-conscious. At least he didn't stare. He seemed to be contemplating something very distant and amusing. Anyway, he asked who I was calling and I shrugged and didn't say anything. Because I knew a phone call would be useless, a futile gesture.

Why?

Because I wanted to call Nettie Halversham.

And yet I didn't want to call her.

There's an old song that goes "What Is This Thing Called Love?" What is it, anyway? I had never given much thought to love before I met Nettie Halversham. And if I had, I would have figured that love was an instant emotion between two people, that if you fell in love with a girl she automatically fell in love with you. Something mutual. As if the universe had been ordered to be that way. All during the time I was a kid, a real kid, like eleven or twelve, I hardly thought above love. I thought it was loving your mother and father. I'd see love stories on television and find them dull and boring. Same with love stories in books and magazines. Later, of course, I'd read love stories to track down the horny parts and they made me wonder how it would be to touch a girl and if being horny was part of being in love, although it seemed to me you needed ultimate respect toward the girl you loved. Like my father's attitude toward my mother: gentle, considerate.

Anyway.

I met Nettie and fell in love with her. Like lightning striking and the thunder was the boom of my heart— talk about song lyrics. I met her when Jackie Brenner and I went to the Hallowell Y one Saturday morning. Fort Delta has the same facilities as the Y, of course, but it was a treat to take a bus into Hallowell and get away from the post. Until a few years ago, my existence and my activities were confined to Delta, which is not as limited as it sounds since Delta is a self-sufficient and self-sustaining community. But I began to get a kind of claustrophobia about two years ago. Unlike some Delta kids who went to school in Hallowell, either at public or private schools, I attended schools on the post: small classes, much individual attention, and educational monitoring my father himself had instituted. So there was a sense of freedom when I went to Hallowell on the bus, not the same old kids, not the same old streets named for famous battles (Tarawa Road, Château

Thierry Avenue), not the same old barracks buildings. That Saturday last August, I met Nettie Halversham in front of the Y. She was standing there with a girl Jackie knew. I looked at her and my knees turned liquid and my stomach felt as though I hadn't eaten for a week. She was not dressed in the usual outfit: jeans and jersey. She wore a blue blouse and a skirt, white with a blue edging. I found myself talking like a crazy man, about all kinds of things, nothing I can recall now, which is just as well. And all the time this happiness was soaring in me because she was looking at me and smiling and laughing at my jokes, whatever they were, and I felt like the most clever, most cool guy in the world. I kept my eyes on her and knew I was in love. I didn't have to run to a dictionary for a definition of the word and I didn't have to rush to a doctor to have my pulse taken. I knew I was in love. Irrevocably. I also figured that she was in love with me, that not just me but *we* had fallen in love, the way it was supposed to happen.

The bus came along and she boarded it with her girl friend and I said, "See you later," as if I was sending her a secret message and she smiled intimately (I thought) and I got her full name and particulars from Jackie and knew that I would call her up and ask her to go out. On a date. We had a lot of socials on the post and I went through the usual horrors of dancing schools and girl-boy birthday parties but I had never had a date before and didn't even know what the hell we would do on a date but I didn't worry about that kind of stuff. I was dealing with destiny here, kismet, fate. And the words of a thousand inane love songs suddenly made sense. *Love will find a way. You are so beautiful to me.*

I called her up, three nights before the seizure of the bus. As I dialed her number, my heart began to beat faster, just like the songs say. When I heard her voice, I melted. Went limp. I told her who I was. She said: "Who?" The word hung in the air like a bell tolling doom. I told her my name again, about meeting her in front of the Y, and she said, "Oh, yes," as if she had just drawn my name from a file cabinet and was confirming my existence. We talked awhile and it was like pumping uphill on my bike. Because she left the talking to me. Oh, she was polite and commented on what I said— dropping in *Yes* or *Gee* or *Huh* like coins in a jukebox to keep the stuff coming—but absolutely volunteering no topics herself. I got desperate. I covered school, the weather, the schedule of activities at the Y, the comparison of summer events between Hallowell and the post, and finally ran out of gas. I was tired of the sound of my own voice but was afraid of stopping because I dreaded the terrible silence that was sure to follow. Finally, I asked her if she'd go to a movie with me. Another pause. And then: "Oh, I don't think so." Those devastating words and the boredom in her voice. She didn't simply say *no*. I'd expected *sorry* at least or *some other time* (after all, she was supposed to be in love with me, wasn't she?) but she merely said: "Oh, I don't think so." As if I'd asked her whether it was going to rain tomorrow. Why couldn't she have lied and said: *I'd love to but. . . .* Instead she made me feel as though I wasn't even a member of the human race.

I hung up after stammering around a bit, sounding like a fool, apologizing, for chrissakes, for having taken up her time and she didn't say anything at all, but let me flounder and thrash around. And then it was over. Now the terrible part: I still loved her. Her face still haunted me. The world was suddenly a wasteland, cold and lonely, like the far side of the moon. And I thought: Hey, what's going on here? Why is it that I love her and she doesn't love me? The world was out of balance, out of kilter, tilted. I realized then why some love songs are sad. *Picking up the pieces of my heart . . .*

Three days later, I was still in ruins, without appetite, anticipating fifty years of this particular agony. When the telephone rang that morning, I rushed to it, thinking crazily that it might be Nettie Halversham, apologizing, ready to have me rush into her arms; it had been a case of mistaken identity, etc.

The caller was my father. Which was unusual. He never called from his office in Delta.

"Ben, are you okay?" he asked.

My God, I thought, he knows: about Nettie Halversham and my agony.

"Fine," I said, the way you say *fine* even if the earth is crumbling under your feet.

And then he told me about the seizure of the bus. And the children.

What bus? What children?

And what did it have to do with me?

This bus: a yellow school bus carrying either sixteen or eighteen children (there was initial confusion about the actual number) from their various homes in Hallowell to a summer camp called Kris Kringle Kamp on the outskirts of town. The bus was hijacked by persons unknown, at least three in number, perhaps more. The bus was intercepted by the hijackers on Route 131 and driven to an old railroad bridge, no longer in use, in a wooded area on the Hallowell-Crenshaw line. A van was also involved in the hijacking and was now on the bridge as well, the van also in control of the hijackers.

The children were between the ages of five and six, preschool age, although some had attended kindergarten or nursery school.

The first communication from the hijackers came

when a ten-year-old Hallowell boy bought a letter into the Hallowell police station. The boy was paid a dollar by a man to deliver the letter. The boy described the man as "old, about forty," with dark everything: hair, clothes, mustache, glasses. The letter was addressed to Brigadier General Rufus L. Briggs, Inner Delta, Fort Delta, Massachusetts. There was a sentence typed on the envelope: *Deliver this message within the hour—it is a matter of life or death.*

This is the essence of what my father told me on the phone, although he was not in possession of all the details at the time. Because Fort Delta and children were involved, he was concerned about me. I told him I was fine and wanted to remind him that I was not, after all, five years old. However, I knew he meant well. I told him I'd been planning to play ball with Jackie Brenner on General Bradley Field. He told me to stay put; that, in fact, he would be sending someone over to watch the house. Meaning: to guard me.

"How about Mom?" I asked, alerted suddenly by the no-nonsense tone of his voice. My mother had left that morning to spend the day in Boston: shopping on Newbury Street in the morning and a matinee in the afternoon.

"I'm sending someone to Boston to track her down," my father said. "Look, Ben, these precautions may seem as if I'm overreacting but I don't want to take chances because . . ."

The *because* hung in the air, surrounded by silence. I hesitated to break that silence, although I knew what should follow the *because*. Because Fort Delta was involved and that probably meant the secret work my father was engaged in.

"But what do the hijackers want, Dad?"

"We don't know yet, Ben. The only message they sent

tells us to stand by for further instructions. That's all I can tell you because that's all I know." I realized my father had never in his life told me that much before about anything. Oh, we talked together, of course, and discussed stuff like the chances of the Red Sox winning the pennant (high hopes in May, sad truth in September) and my marks at school and such, but never anything to do with him, either his work or how he felt about life in general, as if everything aside from baseball or my marks related to his secret duties.

"So stick close to home, Ben. In fact, stay in the house. I know this is tough, but we can't take chances with people like this on the loose," he said.

"Okay," I said.

Then I remembered something that had bothered me during the time we were talking. "Hey, Dad," I said. "You said the message was addressed to General Rufus Briggs. I never heard of him. Who's General Briggs?"

I heard his quick intake of breath and then a silence at the other end of the line. And I thought: My God, General Briggs is *him*, my father, his whatchamacallit, cover name, for chrissakes.

"I can't say any more at the moment, Ben," my father said. "Look, stay put. Someone will be over soon. And don't worry about anything."

I hung up, the telephone perspiring with my transferred sweat.

The bus, the kids, the hijackers, and my father using a cover name all these years at Delta. And: What was Inner Delta?

I realized I hadn't thought of Nettie Halversham for at least three minutes. A kind of record for me that dismal day.

Funny. I can't recall Nettie Halversham's face.

Was it that long ago?

But time is weird, isn't it? It plays funny games. Like this room. It seems as if I have been here forever. But it's been only since last September, hasn't it?

Hasn't it?

To whom do I keep addressing these questions, as if I expected a phantom to sneak in here and answer when I'm not looking?

Speaking of time, it is now 11:15 and they are overdue.

My parents, I mean.

They said they would be here by eleven. Castle is a three-hour drive from Delta. Maybe they had a flat tire. Maybe they started late. Maybe my father has changed his mind and will not come after all.

Maybe I hope he will not come.

Because then I will have sit across from him and look him in the eye. And I know I can't do that. Not yet, not yet.

From where I sit typing, I can see across the quad to the space between Hunter Hall and Old Ivy through which visitors must pass on their way to the dorms or Daniel Webster Hall, where visitors are entertained by students in one of the parlors.

I keep looking up to watch for my mother and father. The snowball fight is over and the quad is deserted. The wind rises occasionally, breaking the covering of snow into soft white rags that fall haphazardly on the ground.

I am typing very slowly now, one word at a time, and between the words and even the letters (I never learned the touch system but must hunt and peck) I look up to wait for them to appear, for *him* to appear.

Hoping he does.

And hoping he doesn't.

And feeling sometime that he's already here in the room with me, watching and waiting.

My father, the phantom.

part
4

Miro hated the waiting. In the airline termi-
nals, in the bus stations, in all the small stuffy
rooms. Or that day in Detroit when they were trapped
in the hotel lobby and waited nine hours, immobilized,
without food or drink, a gun in his hand all that time so
that after a while the gun seemed like a part of him, the
way a sliver in the flesh can become a part of you,
pulsing with pain. There was no pain here in the bus at
least, although it was uncomfortable. The heat was
beginning to gather, and the windows could not be
opened, of course. The children were somewhat subdued but restless, crying out at times, the girl unable to
control them in such moments. When the children
quieted down, the girl sat in the driver's seat, her hands
clenching the steering wheel as she stared into space.

The shock, no doubt.

Miro was glad that he had orders to follow and duties to perform. His first duty had been to apply the plastic sealer to the windows so that they could not be opened except with a great effort. Next, the taping. Miro had applied the masking tape to each window, allowing a thin slit to remain uncovered. In this way, they could look out of the narrow opening without exposing themselves. They would be able to watch the building some one thousand feet away across the chasm where, Artkin said, the soldiers and the police would establish their headquarters. They would also be able to watch the woods on both sides of the chasm for snipers.

Miro had done the taping swiftly and efficiently. The children were a nuisance as he worked. He had to step over them and between them, brushing their legs aside in order to reach the windows. The children looked up at him curiously but with a certain amount of indifference, as if they were watching a scene on television, something that did not affect them at all, something they could tune out if they wished. The effect of the drugs, Miro supposed. Or perhaps American children were already doped with television itself.

As he placed the tape on the last window, he felt a tug at his pants. He looked down. A small blond boy was looking up at him, smiling. The boy did not seem frightened of the mask. He had two missing teeth in the front of his mouth, and the gap in his teeth gave him a clown look. Miro continued to apply the tape and the boy kept tugging at his pant leg. Miro ignored him and hurried to finish the job.

The children were meaningless to Miro. They all looked the same to him: small human beings, without identity, strangers who did not arouse his interest or curiosity. He could make no connection with them. He had never played with children when he was growing up. His only companion had been his brother, Aniel. Aniel had been two years older than he. Neither of them had been children, really. They had scrounged for a living in the refugee camps, although it had been Aniel who had done most of the scrounging, an expert, drifting out into the steaming mornings among the thousands who came and went in the camps and returning later with scraps of food or sometimes clothing—an old jacket, shirts or socks—he had either begged or stolen. Once, Aniel had brought him a small wooden object. Orange. In the shape of an animal.

"What is it?" Miro had asked.

"A toy," Aniel had replied.

The word held no meaning for Miro. He recognized the shape of the toy as an elephant. For some reason, the small object held his attention. He would pretend that the elephant was walking across the desert and that he was riding on it and bad men chased them. And then he awoke one morning and the elephant was gone. He and Aniel searched for it in vain. When Miro had fallen asleep in the abandoned shelter, the elephant had been standing near his face, on the dirt floor. Someone stole it in the night, Aniel had explained to Miro. One of the people with whom they shared the shelter for a while, perhaps.

Miro had accepted the explanation without complaint. Stealing was a way of life. But a dim knowledge took shape within him, just as the wooden object had taken on an animal shape. And the shape of the knowledge was this: Do not seek to own anything, do not try to make anything belong to you, do not look for pleasure in anything. It will be taken from you sooner or later just as you must take from other people.

The boy tugged again at Miro as he finished with the

taping. Miro brushed his hand away and went toward the back of the bus. He walked softly, not wanting to stir the children. He did not want to become involved with them. He wanted to get involved with no one, the girl included. All he wanted to do was follow orders and complete this particular operation. The operation was a worry to him. He didn't feel at ease. He was vaguely disturbed. And he wasn't certain why he felt that way. Was it because Artkin was being secretive about much of it? Artkin who loved to review plans had gone only so far in his review and no further. He had told about the seizure of the bus and the killing of the driver and the drugging of the children and the locks to make the bus secure and even the taping, but nothing about what would happen next. Miro had dared not question Artkin—no one was so foolish as to do that. Artkin had merely said, "Once on the bridge, we wait. We must be patient. But our patience will be rewarded."

Artkin was now in the van with Stroll and Antibbe. Is he outlining the plans to them and ignoring me? Miro asked himself, immediately ashamed of his jealousy. He had been jealous before, simply because he was always the youngest, the uninitiated. His killing of the driver today was supposed to have signified his manhood, his complete acceptance into the brotherhood of freedom soldiers. He looked down at the girl now with resentment. He also resented the dead child who lay here on the back seat, waiting for Artkin to decide what to do about him.

This is why Miro did not like waiting. It gave him too much time to think, to ponder, to wonder about things he should leave to Artkin. He wondered now about the girl, squinting his eyes to see her at the front of the bus. He had tried to engage her in conversation, attempting to follow Artkin's orders, but she had been uncommunicative. Miro pondered what she was thinking. Did she suspect that she would die before this incident was over? Had she seen through Artkin's lies, even though he lied so skillfully? A sudden thought struck Miro. Does Artkin lie to me as well? Have I also been taken in by his skill?

He shook his head as if he could get rid of such a terrible thought that way.

He looked out through one of the window slits. Outside, all was peaceful. The bus was high enough to see over the parapet at the edge of the bridge. The parapet would protect them when they passed from the bus to the van. The building across the chasm was still deserted, without movement. He searched for the glint of sniper rifles in the woods but saw only branches, heavy with summer leaves. A bird cried overhead; he did not recognize the sound. In his homeland beside the river, the old men said that turtle doves and larks circled in the air above the orange trees. He had seen no turtle doves in the United States. No orange trees, either, although Artkin said they grew in southern areas like Florida, where Miro had never gone.

Swiveling his eyes toward the sky again, Miro heard the sound of a helicopter, and his breath caught in excitement. The sound grew louder. He felt the blood begin to pound in his veins, his heart beating rapidly. The helicopter's motor throbbed violently now; it seemed to be on the roof of the bus itself, enveloping the entire bus in its sound.

The waiting was over at last.

Now it could begin.

When Kate heard the sound of helicopter, she had been sitting despondently in the driver's seat, clutching the wheel uselessly, unable to face the children any longer and unwilling to look at the boy Miro. She knew she was doomed. She had known it the moment she saw them put on the masks. The knowledge had sickened her, causing her stomach to lurch with nausea. They had allowed her to see them unmasked. She could recognize them anywhere, identify them, point them out in police lineups, the way it happened on television cop shows. The children perhaps didn't represent a threat to the hijackers; the testimony of five- and six-year-olds probably wouldn't hold up in court. But Kate knew they couldn't afford to let her go. Or let her live.

In an effort to escape the thoughts and the panic they brought, she had moved among the children, tousling hair, stroking cheeks tenderly, speaking to those who weren't completely asleep. Most of the children were still in a kind of half stupor, languid, like limp rags. Now and then a child stirred or sat up, looking around inquiringly. A thin boy with freckles and electric-orange hair tugged at her sleeve. Yawning, he asked, "When are we getting to camp?"

"Soon," she said. "Pretty soon."

He smiled wanly at her and sank into a kind of half sleep, eyelids fluttering.

A girl, blond and blue-eyed, the kind of child who won "Prettiest Baby" contests, looked up at Kate. Her chin quivered, tears spilled on her cheeks.

"What's the matter?" Kate asked gently.

"I forgot my Classie," the child said.

"Who's Classie?"

"Classie's my chraff." She wiped the tears with a small, trembling hand.

"Your what?" Kate asked. She was conscious of the boy Miro looking down at her from where he stood on a seat a few feet away taping the windows.

"My chraff," the child said, sniffing, her nose running now. "I want my chraff."

"She means her giraffe," said a boy who sat slumped next to the girl. He had seemed to be deep in sleep. In fact, his eyes were still closed as he spoke. He was a fat little kid, all roundnesses. Fat cheeks, fat stomach. "She always takes her giraffe with her, but she forgot it today," the boy said.

The girl's face lit up with delight. "You know my Classie, Raymond?" she asked.

"Of course I know her," he answered. His voice was deep, as if coming from a long distance inside his body. He opened one eye and looked around, first at the girl and then at Kate. The eye was bright and alert, gleaming with intelligence. Hardly the eye of anyone drugged. Then he closed the eye again. Kate studied him. She had a feeling that he was sitting there awake, listening, waiting.

"Can we go back and get my Classie?" the girl asked.

"Later, maybe," Kate said. And to change the subject, "What's your name?"

"Monique," the child answered, yawning, rubbing her eyes, her head dropping slowly to one side.

Miro had come down from his perch and advanced toward her now. The mask accented his eyes and his lips. They all looked alike in the masks. His lips had looked sensuous before; now they were merely big and thick. His eyes were magnified: hard and dark and penetrating.

"You don't like the mask?" Miro asked.

"You look repulsive," Kate said, filling her voice with contempt, hoping it disguised her fear, her panic.

Miro drew back. In his mask he had encountered fear and terror before, but never the kind of hatred he saw on the girl's face.

"We will not wear the masks all the time," he said, stumbling a bit over the words. He was uncertain of how to proceed. He wanted to follow orders, win her over, but did not know how to make that look of hate vanish from her face. "We will wear the masks only outside the bus. With the windows taped, there is no need to wear them inside. And they might disturb the children."

Kate turned away. As she did so, she caught sight of the dead child who had been laid across the long rear seat. The body was covered with a piece of bleached linen Artkin had obtained from the van. The child's feet portruded from the covering: tiny green sneakers, almost new, white shoestrings tied neatly, pale green socks bunched at the ankles. Poor Kevin McMann. That was the boy's name. They had allowed Kate to search the boy's body for identification. She'd found his name on a frayed card noting his membership in the Uncle Otto Teevee Club ("Fun For You On Channel 2"). His pockets had yielded few other clues as to who Kevin McMann had been or might have been had he lived. An unwrapped stick of Spearmint gum. An orange crayon. A curled-up length of string, the kind a boy might use to fly a kite or catch a fish.

She wanted to flee the sight of the boy, flee this bus, this bridge; she felt the panic rising in her again, unable to stop the panic just as you can't stop yourself from bleeding. She willed herself to remain outwardly calm at least, and walked toward the front of the bus, sinking into the driver's seat. The sun splashed through the uncovered strip on the windshield, hurting Kate's eyes. I will not cry, she told herself. I will not cry.

Actually, she couldn't remember the last time she cried. Perhaps as a child when she was little Katie Forrester and her mother dressed her up in lace and frills like a child movie star. That had been her first disguise, the first of many. She often wondered where her disguises left off and the real Kate Forrester began. So many disguises. There was the most obvious one, the disguise provided by nature: she was blond, fair-skinned, slender, no weight problems, had managed to avoid adolescent acne. A healthy body with one exception: the weak bladder. That was Disguise Number One: Kate Forrester, healthy young American girl, cheerleader, prom queen, captain of the girls' swimming team, budding actress in the Drama Club. But there were other Kate Forresters, and she wondered about them sometimes. The Kate Forrester who awoke suddenly at four in the morning and for no reason at all couldn't fall back to sleep. The Kate Forrester who couldn't stand the sight of blood—she'd fainted once at a football game when Ron Stanley had been tackled at her feet, his helmet sailing through the air and blood gushing from his head. And the Kate Forrester who was afraid of riding in roller coasters and who oozed with urine between her legs in moments of high excitement. Maybe that was why she refused to let guys touch her and instead kept them beguiled with her wit and charm: knowing how guys could not resist an intimate smile or gentle flattery.

All the Kate Forresters. Were other people like that, she wondered, not simply one person but a lot of them mixed together? Did the real person finally emerge? But suppose that real person turned out to be someone terrible? Or someone who never found love? Isn't that what life was supposed to be—a search for love? She wanted to find somebody to love, to love forever. But who? Her few childhood passions had appeared and gone as swiftly as spring snow melting in the sun. Did she deserve to find love? Was she good enough? That question brought up another Kate Forrester disguise. Kate the manipulator. Who used people shamelessly in, oh, a thousand ways. Getting straight A's from Mr. Kelliher in math and barely lifting a finger to do so but knowing how to smile at him, feign interest, dropping by after school and once, daringly, breathlessly, leaning close to him, letting her breast brush his shoulder. Why had she bothered? She'd always been an excellent student in math. She didn't know why she'd gone out of her way to charm Mr. Kelliher. Just as she didn't know why she'd used the same charm to win the role of Emily in the Drama Club's presentation of *Our Town*. She knew she could play the part, she was certain of her talent. Yet she had played up to David Hart, the director, caressing his ego with tender strokes. Having obtained the role, she'd gone ahead and won the best actress award to prove she deserved the part. One reason she'd wanted the part was to play opposite Gene Sherman. Kate had been enthralled by him, riveted, mesmerized during the first few rehearsals. Until they sat together during a lunch break—and his feet smelled.

My God, she thought later, what do I want? Perfection? What's the matter with me? She wasn't perfect herself, why should she demand perfection from others? What would her friends think if they knew about these secret Kate Forresters, if they could penetrate her disguises?

And then the helicopter, the flutter of the blades, the roar of the motor, drawing closer, filling the air, causing the bus to vibrate. She leaped from the driver's seat toward the doorway. They were saved. Help was coming.

Miro yelled: "Stay in the seat, miss."

But she ignored his words and began pounding on

the door. She tried to wedge her foot in the space where the two locked sections of the door came together. She had to get out there and wave, get the attention of the pilots. And then Artkin loomed in the doorway. With swift, deft movements, he unlocked the door and stepped inside.

"Let me out," Kate cried, struggling as he pushed her toward the driver's seat.

"It's no use, miss," Artkin shouted, an ominous presence in the mask. He grabbed her shoulders roughly, his face only inches from hers. "They will know sooner or later that you are here, if they do not know already."

A high, whining sound now, above the roar of the helicopter, and Kate recognized a police siren, howling and harrowing. "Listen," Artkin said, holding her fast in his grip. "This helicopter now, and a police cruiser and then more helicopters and more cruisers. And army jeeps. Then the television van and the radio cars. This is only the beginning."

He released her, and she groped for the steering wheel for support. She realized the truth now. They were still trapped here despite the helicopters and the policemen and the soldiers.

The children began to cry, awakened violently by the sudden gathering of sounds. Kate looked at them with dismay as they sat up, cheeks tear-stained, clothing rumpled, eyes frightened. *Mommy,* they cried, and *Daddy,* and other words Kate could not discern, words that were the special vocabulary of childhood to express whatever fear or terror they felt, sensing finally that something was askew in the small and safe world they had occupied until this morning.

Now one small child pointed to Artkin's masked face and a howl of terror issued from his small body. His howl touched off a chorus of screams and cries that rivaled the cacophony outside the bus.

"See to the children," Artkin called to Kate. "That is your job. If you cannot do this, you are of no use to them. Or us."

Kate's panties had dried against her body, the weak bladder not having betrayed her for the past hour or so. Now the moisture began to spread and her chafed thighs stung as she walked down the aisle toward the children.

Miro pressed his face to the window, looking out through the narrow opening. Excitement raced in his blood as he observed the scene. He could feel his heart accelerating, pumping energy into every part of his body. This is what he loved: action, movement, things happening. Across the ravine, police cruisers with blue revolving lights had arrived at the building, sirens making the vehicles sound as if they were maddened animals. Two helicopters wheeled in the sky, dipping and slanting, and they, too, were like wild things: birds of prey circling their victims. But we are not victims, Miro thought; they are, everyone out there. Now three army vehicles arrived, two jeeps and a truck. The men in the jeeps bounced forward as the vehicles stopped abruptly. Three men leaped from each jeep, all in uniform, and they ran, crouching, to the building, scurrying, looking as frightened as the children here in the bus. The army truck lumbered to a halt. From beneath its canvas covering soldiers jumped to the ground and then dashed toward the woods. Twenty-five or thirty soldiers, sleek and quick, garbed with camouflage uniforms so that they could blend with the woods and become part of the bushes and trees and scrub brush. Miro knew that these were the snipers.

They disappeared into the protection of the woods so swiftly and easily that one could almost doubt their appearance a moment before.

As abruptly as the sound and movement began, so did it cease. The helicopters wheeled away from the scene, lifting high into the sky as if sucked by a giant's invisible mouth, the sound of their motors fading. The siren howls also faded, then died. The silence was suddenly immense. Even the children became quiet. Miro looked to see the girl moving among them, soothing them, talking gently to them. They reached for her with pleading hands, and it seemed there was not enough of her to go around, to supply them with the reassurance they needed. But that was not Miro's concern at this moment. He looked out at the scene again, searching the woods for movement. He saw, here and there, a branch snapping, a bush jostled. The snipers were already in position, waiting, waiting. The snipers always played the waiting game. Miro spotted two of them.

Artkin positioned himself at the next window.

"The snipers have arrived," Miro said. "They are out there now."

Artkin scanned the scene with an unerring eye. "I know. I have seen five."

Miro was abashed. Why is it when I see only two of something, Artkin always sees three or more? Will I always be the student? Will he always be the teacher?

"At this point," Artkin said, "the snipers are the real danger. Later we must watch for an attack, but for now the snipers are their most potent weapon." Artkin spoke low so that the girl could not overhear. "The snipers are the most patient of men, as they wait. And as they count. They count to see how many of us are here. And they count the openings, the places where they see a bit of flesh here, a bit of clothing there, an eye, a temple, a hand." Miro always marveled at Artkin's concentration and the way he had of lecturing even in the middle of an operation. "So be careful, Miro. Do not expose yourself unnecessarily. And be alert always. Although we are, to some extent, protected from the snipers."

"To what extent?" Miro asked.

They could hear the girl murmuring to the children, calming their fears, reassuring them.

"The message that was sent. The message said that for each one of us who dies or comes to harm a child shall die. They perhaps do not believe this yet. But they will." He glanced at the body of the dead child on the back seat. "In a while, they will know to what extent we will go."

Miro frowned. A question had formed itself in his mind, but he was too timid to ask it. He had never questioned Artkin before, had been content, indeed pleased, to carry out orders.

"Are you troubled, Miro?" Artkin asked.

And Miro saw immediately that he could hide nothing from Artkin.

"This operation," Miro said, and fell silent, turning to the slit in the window once more, afraid that he would see anger in Artkin's eyes at his impertinence.

"What about this operation?" Artkin said. There was no taunt in his voice now.

He did not look at Artkin but spoke the words that were plaguing him. "This operation is different from the others. The others—we struck fast and then ran. The post office explosion in Brooklyn, the confrontation in Detroit. Los Angeles. We did what was necessary. But this is different." He kept his eyes glued to the scene outside, but his words rushed out now. If he were going to be condemned for speaking, then he would speak everything that was in his mind. "We are on a bridge, surrounded. The police out there, and the soldiers. The snipers."

"This is a test of our strength and endurance, Miro," Artkin said, still speaking as a teacher, reasonable, patient. "I agree that we appear to be vulnerable. And that danger is all around us. The woods on both sides of the bridge are dangers. They can bring men in there, snipers and others, more numerous than the trees. And the bridge itself. We are perhaps one hundred fifty feet high and open to possible attack by men climbing the girders under us. At night, especially. But we have Stroll and Antibbe to guard us at night. This is a railroad bridge, Miro, and there is space between the ties to see what goes on below. And we have flashlights and spotlights."

His words did not bring comfort to Miro. Instead, they emphasized the truth of Miro's concern.

"But, most of all, Miro, we have the children. They give us the balance of command. Let the generals and the police chiefs gather in the building across the chasm, let them set up their communications. They are powerless while we have the children."

Perhaps Artkin was right. There had never been reason to doubt him before—why now? The snipers would not dare shoot and risk the lives of the children. Stroll and Antibbe were professionals—they knew their jobs. The building across the ravine was at least a thousand yards away, while behind them there was nothing but the sheer drop to the depths below. Still, Miro was troubled.

"How long will this go on?" he asked.

"Until the demands are met," Artkin said, turning back to the window, studying the scene outside.

"What are the demands?" Miro heard himself asking, taking a deep breath as he spoke, knowing he was taking a desperate chance by asking a question like that.

Artkin did not answer immediately but continued to look at the terrain. Have I sealed my doom? Miro wondered.

"You are growing up, Miro," Artkin said. "I forget sometimes." He looked at Miro, but the boy could not fathom what Artkin was thinking. His eyes, as usual, told nothing. "I am not supposed to forget anything, but I do on occasion. Does the girl bother you? Is that one reason you are troubled?"

That was Artkin: catching you off guard, off balance, striking where you least expect it, from a direction you had not anticipated.

Miro looked down toward the girl. He summoned contempt as he spoke. "She troubles me because she still lives. She was my initiation and cheated me out of it."

"Don't worry. You will have your chance," Artkin said.

So. Artkin had accepted Miro's question without anger or rebuke. Although it was true he did not answer it. And then Artkin said: "In a little while, when things are calmer, I will send Antibbe here to the bus and summon you to the van. And I will explain the operation to you."

Pleasure flooded Miro. Artkin had never taken him into his confidence before. He wanted to express his appreciation to Artkin for the honor. But he could not allow himself to do so. Not in the midst of an operation. And a fighting man does not say things like "Thank you."

The cries of the children began again, a chain reaction. One child cried and others followed, as if fear were contagious, like a disease.

"Help the girl to keep order here," Artkin said. "Win her over. I am planning to give the children more of the drugs. They cannot be managed this way, even with the girl." The clamor of the children continued.

"It is hot in here for them with the windows closed and the door also closed," Miro said.

"They will have to suffer the heat. At least until nightfall." Artkin glanced toward the girl. "Do you think she is capable, Miro?"

"Yes," he said. "For an American girl, she is capable." Miro immediately pondered his statement. Actually, he did not know whether she was capable or not. But she was good with the children, and Miro alone would not know what to do with them.

"Good. But keep her in your sight. Try to determine what she is thinking every moment. She was not part of the original plan—and for that reason she is a danger no matter how helpless or innocent she seems."

"I will watch her every minute."

"Good," Artkin said, touching Miro's shoulder. "I rely upon you. Especially for what happens now."

Miro did not ask: What happens now? He did not want to risk further questions.

Artkin looked toward the dead child on the back seat. "It is time to begin, Miro. Our audience is gathered out there. They are waiting. The last time I looked, a television van had arrived at the building. To have an ending, we must have a beginning. And it begins now."

As if in answer to Artkin's words, the sounds began again, the howl of the sirens and a new siren, the kind that screams *ah-oo, ah-oo,* a two-toned cacaphony that cut through the other sounds like the voice of a machine gone mad.

Gross. But more than gross. It was beyond her most terrible imaginings, so astonishing and—what? She groped for the word and shrunk from calling it into use even as she summoned it: evil. She could think of nothing else to describe the scene before her eyes. And the most terrible thing of all is that she had to keep looking, frozen; she couldn't tear her eyes away from the sight of Artkin, Artkin and the child, Artkin in the mask and the child held aloft, above his head, as if the child were a sacrificial lamb being offered to a mercenary god. The child *was* a kind of sacrifice, Kate realized with horror. And no mercy anywhere, not anywhere in the world.

It had begun a few minutes before, when Artkin had walked with deliberate steps to the back of the bus and had picked up the dead child. She'd been trying to placate the children and finally calmed them down by allowing them to open their lunchboxes and begin to eat whatever their mothers had fixed them for lunch. She'd wanted to save the food for later, when the children got restless. But she also realized that the present moment counted: now, not the next minute, the next hour, the next day. She'd seen Artkin look at the children in annoyance as he talked to the boy Miro at the window. She had to keep them quiet, docile so that Artkin wouldn't feed them any more dope. She had to keep the children from getting on Artkin's nerves. Cripes, she thought ruefully as she held a weeping child on her lap, she had to keep them from getting on her own nerves. She had little experience with kids. She was an only child, had seldom done any baby-sitting. Yet she knew the children were a kind of blessing for her. Worrying about them, she was able to put her own terror aside, at least for a little while. They diverted her panic and channeled her energy into caring for them, keeping her busy, keeping her from thinking about herself.

That was when she looked up to see Artkin pick up

the dead boy and sling him over his shoulder like a slab of meat. The linen cloth slipped partially from the child's body and trailed along the floor.

Artkin stepped out of the bus without glancing in her direction.

She hurried to the front of the bus and looked through the windshield. Miro had left a two- or three-inch strip uncovered across the windshield so that Kate had a clear view of the area outside and the space between the van and the bus. Artkin walked between the two vehicles and stood near the parapet. He held the child aloft, above his head, his hands supporting Kevin McMann's neck and the back of his knees. Artkin's own back was arched. His masked face was raised to the sky. He offered the child to that same sky. The child's arms hung limply in the air, dangling lifelessly.

A silence fell on the scene, more abrupt than the earlier silence. The *ah-oo, ah-oo* of the siren was cut off in mid-scream, as if strangled by an unseen hand. The children on the bus sat like small robots whose motors had run down. Or, as if they sensed somehow, as children often do, that this was a moment to be quiet, to wait, to remain silent.

Artkin began to turn around, slowly, deliberately, his arms stretched high, the child still held aloft, turning, turning, quicker now, stepping up the movement, as if he were dancing to some compelling music nobody else could hear. The silence continued, both within the bus and outside. Why don't they shoot him? Kate thought. There are cops out there and soldiers, with guns and rifles. Shoot him!

"They will not shoot him," Miro said, his voice loud in Kate's ear even though he was whispering. He had crowded close to her to view the scene through the limited space. She turned to him, horrified. She'd spoken aloud without knowing she did so. Christ, she thought, I'm coming apart at the seams.

"I'd shoot him," she said, needing to hear the sound of her voice to restore her footing in the world. "I'd blast him off the face of the earth."

"They cannot take that chance, miss. The demand we sent—it said that for every one of us who is harmed, a child will die."

While Artkin continued to whirl.

Quicker now, swifter.

Turning and turning, a dance of depraved delight. The child's dangling arms swinging wildly as Artkin whirled. The spinning was building momentum now, and Kate feared that Artkin would lose his hold on the child, who would go spinning off into the air, over the side of the bridge, falling to the river below. But the child was dead, of course. The child could no longer be harmed, thank God. He was beyond reach of Artkin's madness.

"He's a madman," Kate said.

"No, miss. Not a madman. He knows exactly what he is doing. He is showing them that we do not go by the rules of others, the laws of others, and that life is not precious to us. Not a child's, not our own."

Kate did not wish to witness the scene any longer. She tore her eyes away from Artkin's dance and looked toward the children. They looked back at her quietly, trustingly. So defenseless, so innocent, so vulnerable. And children first of all: one girl sucked her thumb, a boy scratched his buttocks, another boy's face was sticky with jam from his sandwich.

She moved toward the children, feeling anew her responsibility toward them.

"What happened out there, miss," Miro said, "could have been worse."

"How?" she asked, keeping her voice cold, such a small gesture of defiance.

"It could have been—" And the boy did not say more.

Kate shriveled inside but maintained an outward composure. She wouldn't give in to him. She knew what the boy had almost said: it could have been *you*.

By the time the children had finished their lunches, the sirens began to sound again, and the mechanical flutter of the helicopter could be heard once more.

She hated herself for asking, but she couldn't help it. "Has he stopped that crazy dance?" she asked the boy.

"It was not crazy and it was not a dance," Miro said. "But yes, it has stopped."

"What did he do with the child?"

"He gave him back," Miro said.

He spared her the agonizing *how*.

"He lowered the child by a rope to the bottom of the bridge. We are not animals, after all."

Yes, you are, Kate thought, yes you are.

part
5

My father and me. In confrontation. Six
guns at sunset in the western town, the shadows
slanting long over the false-front street, the fake street
we saw the time my mother and father and I visited
Universal City in Hollywood. Not Hollywood really,
Burbank, California. Everything fake out there, even
Hollywood, which isn't really Hollywood but a lot of
other places. Just as I am a fake, here, sitting at the
typewriter, typing for the sake of typing, something to
keep my fingers busy and my mind distracted.

Anyway.

We have just had our first meeting, me and my
father, since the Bus. Me at one end of the sunset town,
him at the other. The bad guy is supposed to be in black,
but I am actually wearing jeans, a blue Castle T-shirt

under a beige cardigan sweater that my mother was disgraced to see is threadbare at the elbows. My father should have been in white, like all the good guys, but he was wearing his tweed jacket and gray flannel pants and gray turtleneck. My mother jokingly calls this his professor outfit, claiming that it makes him feel as if he is still on the campus of good old New England U. in Boston. Which may be true.

Waiting for somebody to make the first draw, counting silently. But nobody did. Although some guns were fired.

You know what I'm doing at the moment, don't you?

Some verbal sleight of hand, but I am trying to deceive myself not anyone else.

I am playing the warmup act before the main event comes on, trying to come up with funny songs and dances and some jokes.

Like Henny Youngman.

First man: Any cops around here?

Second man: No.

First man: Stick 'em up.

I am laughing to keep from crying.

And typing to keep my hands from crawling like big white spiders all over the place.

And keeping my lips sealed, my mouth clenched tight so that the scream I keep inside does not escape and fill the room with its anguish.

*   *   *

The asterisks again.

Denoting the passage of time.

But only a few minutes. Three, four at the most.

Time going slowly, bent out of shape like a Dali watch.

But a good thing so that I can control myself.
There. That's better:
My hand has stopped shaking.

My father has stepped out of the room. To use the john at the end of the corridor. He is taking some kind of blood-pressure pill and there is no water here in the room, so he excused himself a few moments ago to find a paper cup and water.

He also said that he must check in with Dean Albertson: something about a lecture he has been asked to give during the winter.

He also said he must telephone my mother, his wife, to let her know he arrived here in good time.

Excuses, of course.

He really wanted to get out of here, out of this room, away from this person who is by an accident of birth his son.

I can't blame him.

"Please wait," he said. "I'll be back in a little while."

So I am waiting.

I also should get out of here and make my pilgrimage to Brimmler's Bridge, but I will wait for him, keep my word, honor my father.

Besides, I would not want to do anything rash so soon after seeing him because then he would blame himself and wonder: What did I say? what did I do?

So, I'll wait.

Wait for him to get back.

And wait until later for my appointment at the bridge.

But I must keeping typing.

I lied before when I said that I never learned the touch system but must hunt and peck. I wrote that down so that I could justify looking out at the window so often to see if my father was approaching.

I am really a terrific typist. Between 60 and 70 words a minute, one of the bonuses of that exclusive concentrated school at Delta.

* * *

Let me say how I first saw my father when he finally arrived today. It was exactly 11:25 A.M. when I saw him emerge into the quad. My mother wasn't at his side. I didn't recognize him immediately. Oh, I recognized him, I suppose: he was six feet tall, as usual; he walked with his head slanted to one side, as usual, as if he were listening to something far away.

But there was something else I didn't recognize. Something new about him and so strange that I could not pin it down right away.

An air of tentativeness about him.

He was walking at his usual pace, not fast and not slow, but—different.

As if he were walking for the first time in a long time.

As if he were breaking in a new pair of legs.

Or walking on stilts.

And there was also a fragility about him.

He came across the quad as if he were made of glass and was afraid that he would shatter into a million pieces if he bumped into something.

His face: a blank.

I couldn't make out his features at that distance and I imposed my own version on his face. Which was terrifying, of course.

As I watched his progress across the quad, walking fragilely on the new snow, I thought: This is what I have done to him. This is what my action on the bridge did to him.

I sat and waited, although I wanted to run out of there.

If he had come this far to see me, how could I deny him this last look?

My mother was right: he looked terrible. Gaunt, Abraham Lincoln but without the height or the beard. I never realized how deep in the sockets his eyes were set. Or had they sunk to those depths since I saw him last?

I greeted him at the door and we shook hands, firmly but awkwardly. We probably had not shaken hands a half dozen times in our lives.

"Ben," he said, and immediately looked away, glancing around the room, commenting on its size and roominess, etc., and I admired him for the heartiness he had injected in his voice. My father, the actor.

Finally, he swiveled and looked at me. Really looked. As if he were studying me. I wondered what he hoped to see—the kid I'd been a long time ago when a child is innocent, without blemishes? Or was he seeing me as the kid who used to strike out in the Little League games, although I did hit a triple once in a crucial game and scored two runs and heard for the first (and only) time the cheers of a crowd? Or was he seeing me as I was last summer before the Bus and the Bridge? Before the betrayal.

"Well," he said, standing back and still inspecting me. "I see you've gained weight, Ben, and I've lost some."

"Great food here," I said, automatically, meaninglessly. Because I hadn't gained any weight that I know of, although I must admit I don't go running to the scale every day like some denizens of the gym around here.

And then I realized that it was going to be *that* kind of conversation, filled with interpretations, hidden meanings, second guessing on what was said, the search for a tone of voice and what it means, ad infinitum. And I told myself: patience, get through it, play the game, act the part of the dutiful son, follow his lead and try not to hurt him anymore.

And now it was my turn to say something because I realized a great big silence had developed in the room, so deep and awful that it was suffocating. As usual, my mouth began to work and the words started to come out, the way it happened that day I met Nettie Halversham and talked nonstop, and I went on and on about Castle and the guys and Elliot Martingale and the classes and, Jesus, I thought somebody better stop me before I lost my breath and fell in a dead faint at his feet. Finally, I wanted to shatter that awful stare of his, the expression I could not interpret. And out of me erupted the words that had hounded my days and nights since last August.

"Was Inner Delta saved, Dad?"

You couldn't find the answer to that question in the newspapers or in the television newscasts. I couldn't ask anyone else about it, not even my mother. The only one was my father. I had never heard of Inner Delta before the hijacking and I had never heard of it since.

"It was saved, Ben," he said. "Oh, there was some damage, of course. The problem with an operation like Inner Delta is that it depends entirely on secrecy, and that's what the hijackers were counting on—making it public, focusing publicity on it, and therefore rendering it useless. Plus their other demands." His voice trailed off. I knew how difficult it was for him to speak of things he had been pledged to be silent about.

*   *   *

He had first explained Inner Delta to me on the afternoon of the hijacking. He came to the house after lunch and told the bodyguard to wait outside. I had just finished a tuna fish sandwich—it was tasteless because Nettie Halversham had made my entire world tasteless, odorless, and colorless—and I offered to make him one. He said that he did not have time to eat, that he had come home for a few moments to talk to me.

"Did you locate Mom?" I asked.

"Yes, in Boston. She's staying with Sarah Thomspon in Weston. I want her to remain there today and tonight at least." He hesitated. "There have been reports of possible bombings at the entrances to Delta and I don't want her on the highways in this area. She'll be safer with Sarah." Sarah was an old school chum of my mother's, and Weston is a suburb of Boston, a few miles west of the city.

For the first time I sensed the drama going on about me. The radio had been sketchy about the hijacking, interrupting the record sessions with bulletins that told us nothing, really. And television had continued with its endless daytime game shows. But seeing my father tense and pale, hearing him talk of possible explosions and providing for my mother's safety, gave the day's events sudden immediacy in my life. I also looked at my father for the first time in my life as not my father: General Rufus Briggs. . . .

Maybe he saw that look.

Because he said: "I'm going to confide in you, Ben. And tell you as much of what's going on as I can. Within the limits to which I am confined. As you know, some unidentified men are holding a busload of children hostage. That happened about nine A.M. today. We have since received their demands. The demands were made by letter, the letter delivered by a private messenger service out of Boston."

"What do they want, Dad?"

"They've made three demands," he said, relaxing now for the first time, as if he were preparing to put his thoughts in order, not only to provide me with information but to sort out his own feelings about it all. "Number one, they're demanding the release of fifteen so-called political prisoners serving various sentences in this country. Two, they're asking for ten million dollars in cash. Three, they're demanding the dismantling of what is known to some people as Inner Delta. By dismantling, they mean make a public confession of its existence, reveal the names of its agents around the world, recall them from their assignments." He paused, sighed, rubbed his neck as if he were trying to loosen the tension there.

I didn't dare breathe. Or move. I had a feeling he had forgotten I was there, and if I did anything to remind him of my presence he would instantly shut up and go off to Inner Delta, wherever that was.

"We have until tomorrow morning at nine to meet the demands. Or, they say, the children will die, one by one." He looked at me again and, again, seemed to react to the expression on my face. "I'm not telling you any deep secrets, Ben. Most of this will be on the newscasts later in the day. We're trying not to turn this into a media circus but we can't keep it all under wraps."

"Can you meet the hijackers' demands, Dad?" I asked.

"From a practical standpoint, Numbers One and Two can be met. Those political prisoners could be released without any threat to the public or great uproar. They're not members of a conspiracy or anything. They have a wide range—from a trio involved in arson during a civil rights demonstration back in the Sixties to a pathetic character who threw a homemade bomb on the lawn of the White House. The bomb never exploded.

"The money isn't a problem, either. Ten million dollars is a drop in the bucket as far as government spending goes. It may take some doing to round up that amount in a short time, but it's not a major concern.

"The third demand is the stickler, Ben. Inner Delta. I can't tell you what Inner Delta is—I can only say that its work is secret, highly specialized and important in the defense of this nation. I have given my life to it. And, in a sense, gave you and your mother's lives to it by bringing you to Delta. And the dismantling of Inner Delta is the major reason why the children have been abducted. We are convinced of that. The release of the prisoners and the demand for the money are smokescreens. The major issue here is Inner Delta."

We were sitting in the living room and it was as familiar as my own face when I look into a mirror. But suddenly the familiarity took on a strangeness. Because of what my father was saying. Some kids had been hijacked and might be killed, and a secret U.S. agency was involved. And suddenly so were we—my father, my mother, and me. Not directly involved, of course. And yet, I reminded myself, there was a bodyguard standing outside and my mother was being detained out of town because the highways were dangerous for her to travel. I took a deep breath and felt a little dizzy, giddy, as if I were living in one of those little glass scenes that you shake to start the snow whirling around. There was no snow here, but our world was shaken up. I weighed the one question I wanted to ask my father but dared not. *Are you General Briggs, Dad?*

My father placed both hands on his knees and looked

directly at me again. He seemed more relaxed now. That old hands-on-his-knees move always was a prologue to some decision, it seemed. Like: let's go out and throw the ball around. Or: why don't the two of us take in a movie? Now he said: "So there you have it, Ben. I wanted you to know the truth. There's going to be a lot of stuff on radio and television and in the newspapers. A lot of it will be garbled and wrong. Some of it we will mean to be wrong. We have to guard Inner Delta. And it's going to mean withholding certain information or"—he sought the right word, one he wanted me to hear, and found it—"or obscuring the information. But I don't want you to be confused by anything you hear. I've told you the facts of the case. I want to assure you that your mother's safe and so are you. But we have to take all precautions, as a matter of procedure, Ben."

But there was one question I had to ask, whether it involved secrecy or not. And I asked it:

"Are you going to meet the demands of the hijackers, Dad?"

He didn't answer for a long moment and looked tired suddenly.

"We have to wait for official policy to be announced," he said. "But I can't envision giving in to the demands of hijackers. This would set a precedent that could touch off mass hijackings, the way it's happened in other countries." He shook his head.

"But what happens if you don't give in?" I asked, thinking of the kids on the bus and remembering all the hijackings in the world in which innocent people, including kids, died.

"We're not completely helpless, Ben," he said. "We've launched one of the most massive investigations in the history of our country. It involves thousands at all levels of law enforcement. Federal, state, and local authorities are at work. We have clues—the method being used by the hijackers. There are informers out there, ready to give information. We've set up a national center to receive and correlate information. It's a race against time, of course, but we've already made progress. Meanwhile, we have to prepare to bargain. Or make a pretense of bargaining. And there are other possibilities I can't go into now. Anyway, we are proceeding on the assumption that we won't have to meet the demands and the children will be saved."

He stood up then, slowly, achingly, as if his own body was making demands he was finding difficult to meet. He sighed again. "One child has already died, Ben."

"They killed him?" I asked, stunned. Were there really people in the world who killed children?

"We aren't certain yet. One of the hijackers lowered the body from the bridge. After doing a crazy dance with the child in his arms."

"Was the hijacker in plain sight? Why didn't someone shoot him?"

"Their messages said that a child would die for every one of the hijackers who was killed, either by sniper fire or any other way. We can't take chances, Ben. And we're not sure about the death of the child. There was no evidence of violence on his body. It appeared that he had been drugged. They're carrying on tests right now. But the fact remains—a child has already died. And there are fifteen more on the bus, plus the girl who was driving it." He came across the room and placed his arm around my shoulder. He had not touched me in years, except to shake hands on occasion, like when my report card was unusually good. "I've got to get back," he said. "But I'll keep in touch. Your mother will be through to you on the phone a little later. We're arranging special lines. But stay in the house, Ben. And be patient. Okay?"

"Okay."

He stood there in his proper shirt and tie, the colors subdued, the style muted, touches of gray like small pale slivers in his hair. He did not look like a general and he did not look like a man heading a secret agency with operatives all over the world. All that seemed impossible. It seemed almost impossible, too, that a bunch of kids whose lives were in peril had anything to do with me, with us, here in our house on Fort Delta, which always had seemed to be a quiet and placid place. Even boring sometimes. Again, I had the feeling that someone had turned our world upside down, topsy-turvy, and the pieces had not yet settled into place. I wondered if they ever would.

Let us pause here for a second, not a pause for station identification but another kind of identification: where I am, who I am.

For a minute there, typing madly, I was back home on that afternoon of the hijacking. With my father. And now I'm back in this room and my fingers are perspiring from all this typing and they keep slipping off the keys. I have a pain in my back from sitting hunched at the typewriter.

He has been gone for more than a half hour.

He has been gone longer than he stayed in the room talking to me.

It's hard to believe he was really here.

He didn't do much talking. And he barely looked at me, stealing quick glances once in a while when he thought I wasn't looking. And our conversation was a failure. Oh, he told me that Inner Delta was saved with only minor damage, but he volunteered no further information. Secrecy time again. We are back at *Go*.

I asked him why my mother, his wife, had not accompanied him.

He said she has a touch of flu, nothing serious, but she preferred not to take the long trip. She would call me later today. He was planning to stay overnight and had arranged for a room at the Pompey Inn. Perhaps we might have dinner there, it seemed a decent place. He had returned here as a guest lecturer on occasion and also for a class reunion or two, and the old school still seemed like a fine place. Some of his happiest days had been spent here. There were changes, of course. Most of his old teachers were gone, but life was like that, always changing. I didn't mention old Mr. Chatham. I listened mostly, wondering how long he could go without looking at me. He looked everywhere in the room except at me. I wondered: Am I really here? If he finally looks at me, what will he see?

Finally, he fled this room, with his excuses.

I see him now.

He and Dean Albertson are walking across the quad together. Parting now, my father waves to him. Dean Albertson is carrying a Christmas wreath. I have forgotten that Christmas is coming soon.

Is Christmas the time of year that Catholics must go to confession, or is that some other holy day? I'll have to ask Donateli, who seems to be a Catholic. Maybe that's what I need. Not to be a Catholic, but to confess. Because after confession comes forgiveness, doesn't it? What do they call it? Absolution. And yet I realize that I don't have to confess. He already knows what I've done. On the bridge. But I still have to ask forgiveness. If I do, will he forgive me?

He's on his way to the room now.
I know. I can feel him coming.
And now I need to flee, get out of here, and leave.
Hide.
But is there any place to hide?

part
6

"The bathroom," Kate said.

"What about the bathroom?" Miro asked.

"The kids. One of them has to go. And that means all of them will have to go eventually."

"There is no bathroom," Miro said. "They cannot go. There is no place for them to go. This is a bus."

"*You* tell them. You can't stop kids from going to the bathroom," Kate said, taking a small pleasure in this bit of defiance.

Miro grimaced in exasperation. His first responsibility, and he was faced with this kind of problem. A foolish problem. He had schooled himself to remain intact, not to give in to the demands of the body. It was one of the things you learned. He looked at the children with distaste. He did not want to go to Artkin with this problem. He would look foolish in Artkin's eyes.

"Well, what you are going to do about it?" Kate asked, pleased at Miro's discomfort.

Miro turned to the children. "Who needs—" He waved his hand to complete the sentence. He hated these crude and coarse American words. The children stared at him blankly. "Who needs the bathroom?" Miro managed to say.

A girl held up her hand. "I do." Another hand shot up. And another.

"There is no place for them to go," Miro said to Kate furiously. He swiveled toward the children once more. "No one can go," he yelled at them.

To emphasize the words, he drew on the mask and regarded them menacingly.

A little girl stepped into the aisle. A stream of urine traced a course down her leg and spread onto her blue sneakers, turning the powder blue a deeper hue. She began to cry.

At that moment, Artkin entered the bus. He took off his mask. The child continued to cry, her sobs getting louder and louder, and the urine continuing to stream down her leg. "What is going on?" Artkin asked.

"The kids. They need to go to the bathroom. And he says they can't," Kate replied, nodding toward Miro, sorry for the poor child who stood there soaked in her own urine. Kate was familiar with that feeling.

Artkin ignored Kate and spoke directly to Miro. "These things cannot be helped. There's a plastic pail in the van. Bring it here." And to Kate, he said: "You have another duty, miss. You are in charge of the pail."

Miro shot Kate a look of triumph.

"When the pail needs to be emptied, ask Miro's permission and he will allow you to empty it outside,"

Artkin said. Addressing the children, he said: "In a moment, all of you will be able to go to the bathroom. It will not be like your homes but pretend it is an adventure. The lady here will assist you."

Later, Artkin came onto the bus with two brown paper bags in his hand.

Kate recognized what they were—and what they meant. "No," she cried out, leaping to her feet.

Artkin stopped in his tracks. Miro held his breath. No one ever protested to Artkin that way; no one ever said no to him.

"Out of the way, miss," Artkin said.

"I don't want the children drugged again," Kate said. "It's too dangerous."

"It is not your concern, miss," he said patiently, but it was the kind of patience that carries a warning: do not go too far.

"You said the children are my responsibility," Kate said. "And they are. For as long as they're on the bus."

"Then you should be happy that we have the drugs to keep them quiet. So that they won't know what's going on," Artkin said. "It will be a long, hard day for everyone. Perhaps longer than a day. Two days, three. The drugs will keep them sleepy. It will help them, if anything. You should be happy that we have the drugs."

"But one of them died," Kate reminded him. "The drugs killed one of them."

"An accident. The child had a weak heart, perhaps. An unfortunate reaction. But the others showed no bad effects."

"There's no guarantee," Kate said, knowing her objections were futile, her voice faltering now.

"There is no guarantee of anything in this life, miss," he said, brushing past her now, taking the candy out of a bag and holding it up for the children to see. The children responded immediately, holding up their hands: *Want some. . . . Me, too. . . . Chocolate. . . .*

Miro sighed, softly, with relief. The girl had lost the argument, as Miro knew she would. But she had defied Artkin again and Artkin had not retaliated. Yet, Miro knew that Artkin had no cause for retaliation. The girl was doomed, anyway.

So began a time at mid-afternoon when the children came under the influence of the drugs. From this time on, the children were doped and dazed, sluggish with sleep, limp and listless. They ceased to have identities. Earlier, Kate had gone among them, asking their names, rousing those still slumbering, trying to make some kind of contact with them. The names had individualized the children for Kate, but she still got some of them mixed up. There was Monique, of course, still longing for her Classie, and the freckled, red-haired boy who was Alex. Karen with tiny earrings in her pierced ears and Chris who was a boy but might have been a girl with his bangs and flowing brown hair. Raymond with his eyes still closed. Kimberly who wore steel-framed glasses, one lens cracked. Alison and Debbie and Kenneth and Jimmy, whom she had not yet sorted out and so still got their names confused. Mary in pigtails, now unraveling. The two sisters, Ginny and Patty, who looked utterly unlike sisters, for Ginny was pale and delicate, almost transparent, and Patty was dark and robust. P.J., thin-faced and sad-eyed, who had hardly uttered a word (someone else had volunteered his initialed identification), and Tommy who wore horn-rimmed glasses that seemed permanently smudged and probably contributed to his perpetual squint.

With the latest dose of drugs, the children had become a drowsy, dozing, pathetic gathering of arms and legs, heads and shoulders: bodies only, not people. Once in a while, an individual rose from the mass. A child would come awake in a dazzling moment of clarity and truth, suddenly thrust into horror: *Where am I? Where's Mommy? Where's Daddy? I want to go home.* Kate would soothe the waking children, holding them in her arms, stroking their foreheads, caressing their cheeks, murmuring sweet nothings until the flash of wakefulness passed and they sank again into sleep, eyelids fluttering, sometimes a bubble of spittle in the corner of a loose and languid mouth.

The bus seated forty persons, so there was plenty of room. Kate had allowed the children seats of their own unless someone wanted to stay with a friend. Some had brought along teddy bears or other stuffed toys. Ginny and Mary and P.J. clung to their security blankets or, rather, the remnants of them, P.J. passing his patch of blanket caressingly across his cheek as he dozed. As Kate watched them dozing or sleeping, caught in a world without time or tempo, a small dim part of her was grateful for the drugs. To some extent, they helped. The drugs spared the children the knowledge of their predicament, held at bay the nightmare of being hostages. Drugged, they didn't know the dangers that surrounded them. They wouldn't miss their mothers and fathers so badly.

Kate thought of her own mother and father. God, what were they thinking? She realized she had barely given them a thought since the takeover of the bus. Maybe she had purposely blocked them out of her mind, just as she tried not to think of the kids at school. Thoughts panicked her; so did memories. She had to concentrate on the bus and the children, here and now.

She had to stop the tendency to push panic buttons.

Passing down the aisle, Kate noticed Raymond, the plump cheeks, the closed eyelids that moved sometimes. She was convinced that the boy was not really sleeping, that he was faking it.

He was alone in the seat, his head reclining against the taped window. She sat down beside him.

"Raymond," she said.

He didn't answer. She could hear his breathing, saw the gentle rise and fall of his chest.

"Raymond, you can't fool me. I know you're not sleeping."

"I know," he said, eyes still closed.

"Why are you pretending to sleep?" she asked, whispering now.

"I didn't eat the candy," Raymond said. His deep old man's voice.

"Why not?"

"My mother doesn't allow me to eat candy. Or chew gum. Even sugarless gum. She says it's bad for my teeth and I'll thank her someday."

He opened his eyes. They were bright and alert, transforming his fat baby face into the visage of an intelligent little human being. Like a grown-up person in miniature. He glanced toward the front of the bus where Miro stood guard. Leaning toward Kate, he whispered: "After I heard you talking to the men, I knew they'd put poison or dope or something in the candy. I told Monique not to eat any but she did, anyway. Then I pretended to sleep, like the others. I thought they'd be mad at me and punish me if I didn't sleep."

Poor kid, Kate thought, alone all this time, and awake.

"Is Kevin coming back?" Raymond asked.

"Oh, Raymond," she said.

She had dreaded this moment when one of the children would inquire about Kevin McMann. Until now, none of the children had said anything about Kevin, had shown no curiosity about him, why he had lain on the back seat apart from the others, why Artkin had carried him out of the bus. They had been doped up, of course, their senses dulled. Probably children were like adults who blinded themselves from the truth by pretending it did not exist. Or maybe little kids had no loyalties except to their mothers and fathers; other kids slipped in and out of their lives without leaving anything behind, not even memories. Whatever the reason, Kate had been relieved at their lack of questions. But leave it to Raymond. Bright and alert Raymond.

"Kevin isn't coming back, Raymond."

She saw panic flash in Raymond's eyes. She knew she couldn't tell him the truth.

"Kevin got sick. Maybe the stuff in the candy made him sick. So the man took him to the van out there. There's a bed in the van. He's better off there."

"They shouldn't give children stuff that can make them sick," Raymond said.

"I know," Kate said.

"They're bad men," Raymond said, his old man's voice suddenly frail. "Is somebody coming to save us?"

"I hope so, Raymond," Kate said, searching for the right words. "We're not alone, you know. There are policemen and soldiers out there. They've surrounded the bridge. I'm sure they're going to get us out of here."

"You didn't eat the candy, did you, Kate?"

"No, I want to be awake and alert."

"I want to be awake and alert, too," he said.

She touched his fat pink cheek. She felt oddly comforted, and didn't know why. Maybe it was discovering an ally on the bus, even though he was only five years old.

"Maybe I can help you," he said.

"Maybe," Kate answered, to make him feel good.

Suddenly, Raymond closed his eyes and his body went limp, his head drooping to one side. A moment later, Kate felt the presence of Miro nearby. His leg brushed her arm as he passed. She shivered slightly, although it was warm on the bus, the heat gathering as the day progressed. Miro took up his station near the door again. Kate looked down at Raymond. He had sensed Miro's approach and had immediately feigned sleep. He was a smart little kid. The situation suddenly presented possibilities to Kate. A faint strand of hope. The boy wasn't drugged; she knew something the hijackers didn't know. Perhaps the boy could help in some way. Sometimes a kid could do something an adult couldn't do, squeeze into a place an adult couldn't squeeze. Her mind raced. Maybe other things. The important thing was this: Artkin and Miro and the others didn't know.

She bent her head toward Raymond.

"Keep pretending," she whispered. "Maybe you can be my helper. I'll come and talk to you later."

Raymond lifted his face toward Kate. One eye opened and closed.

The wink made Kate smile.

Kate's thighs were chafed and irritated.
She thought: I've got to get out of these, pants.
The panties were damp, and the dampness was acid
eating her flesh.

The children were still subdued, dozing in the
dimness of the bus. The day had turned cloudy. The
absence of sun and the blocking out of light by the tape
gave the interior of the bus an aspect of twilight. This
fake dusk softened the sharp edges of things, and Kate
found herself growing drowsy on occasion. The afternoon was at a standstill, the bus surrounded by silence
except for the occasional howl of a siren or throb of a
hovering helicopter.

"How long will this go on?" Kate had asked Artkin
when he had looked into the bus a few minutes ago,
something he did periodically despite Miro's presence.
It seemed she had asked Artkin that question a million
times, and a million times he had answered: "No one
knows. We must be patient." In one way, she wanted
this standstill to go on and on. Each moment that passed
gave her a sense of having survived this long. She was
afraid of what would happen if some kind of action took
place. The thought haunted her: They can't afford to
let me survive. They will kill me first. She had lived with
that knowledge for such a long time now—time, she had
learned, has nothing to do with a clock on a wall or a
watch on your wrist—that the shock and horror was
muted, had become part of the nature of her existence.
And, mostly, she refused to think about it but kept

herself busy moving among the children, holding one or another, or peeking out the window looking for some sign of encouragement out there. She drew comfort passing Raymond's seat and patting his head. Sometimes, he opened that one bright gleaming eye. Other times, he was quiet, and she hoped that he slept.

As for Miro, he was a brooding presence in the bus. His eyes followed her but looked elsewhere when she turned toward him. He often studied the outside terrain with a concentration that amazed Kate. He could stand in one position forever, it seemed, unmoving and yet somehow relaxed, as if he'd had years of training. Maybe he had. He also stood at the doorway of the bus on occasion, the door open, the lock dangling, drinking in the outside air. The air dissipated the smells of urine and perspiration that had accumulated in the bus. Kate was afraid her own urine had contributed to the rancidness of the air. She longed for a shower. Or just to wash herself down there. And she had to take off these pants.

Miro was standing just outside the doorway, facing away from Kate. She made her way to the back of the bus, touching a child here and there as she passed. With one hand gripping the top of a seat for balance, Kate removed her jeans. Her wallet slipped to the floor. She let it lay there for the time being. She stepped out of her jeans. Her legs felt cool even in the heat of the bus, free of the denim. She glanced over her shoulder: the children still slept and Miro was still out of sight. She drew down the panties, the nylon damp on her flesh. She stepped out of them. Standing there for a moment, she let the air caress her irritated flesh. She rubbed herself there, as if she could soothe her skin that way, wipe away the chafing. Turning slightly, glancing over her shoulder, she saw Miro at the far end of the bus. He was looking at her, suspended, caught in mid-motion, one foot on the top step near the driver's seat. Frozen. He wore the mask, which always emphasized his eyes. His eyes now were huge and startled. She could see them even at this distance. There was also something else in those eyes. She knew that look.

Furious for allowing herself to be discovered this way, naked buttocks exposed, Kate groped for her jeans and pulled them on with trembling fingers. When she looked again, Miro was gone. Vanished. As if he had never been there at all.

Spotting the wallet on the floor, she stooped and picked it up. The wallet, getting frayed with use, a birthday gift from her mother last year. As she began to slip it into her pocket, she remembered the key in the change compartment among the loose nickels and dimes. The key to the bus that her uncle had given her a few weeks ago, which she hadn't bothered to attach to the chain holding her other keys. This morning, her uncle had left his own key in the ignition when he'd gone into the house to ask her to take his run to the children's camp. Kate took out the key; it was cool on her flesh. She clutched it tightly, wanting to confirm its presence, feel its reality. She looked around apprehensively. No Miro. The children sleeping. Beautiful. She removed one sneaker and placed the key inside. She slipped the sneaker on and felt the key slide toward the front of the sneaker. The key nestled between her toes. It felt good as she walked to the front of the bus, as she touched the children. I've got a secret, she thought with delight, almost giddy. Not only a secret but a weapon. The key was a weapon to be used against the hijackers. The key could start the bus, and the bus could take them out of here. She went by Raymond. Another secret: Raymond who did not sleep, Raymond who was bright and alert.

Her panties were bunched in her hand. Kate slipped them into her back pocket. She thought of Miro and the way he had looked at her when she'd stood there practically naked. She remembered the look in his eyes. No girl could ever mistake that look. Maybe she had another weapon in her small pathetic arsenal.

One of the children cried out, a nightmare cry that split the silence. She went to the child—Monique emerging from a bad dream—and murmured sweet soothing sounds. Sweet, because maybe she and the children were not so hopeless or helpless after all.

Miro entered the bus and removed the mask. His skin was hot and flushed. The girl was bending over one of the children, absorbed in the child. He resented the children. They were an additional burden. Their restlessness got on his nerves. Their cries often disturbed his quiet moments of reverie, memories of himself and Aniel long ago. The children demanded the girl's constant attention, which made it difficult for him to approach her, to win her confidence. Artkin had said the girl was his responsibility, but he felt as though he was not doing his job properly. She eluded him all the time, refused to meet his eyes, sought refuge in the children.

He watched the girl now, looking at the jeans covering the flesh he had seen exposed and unclothed a few moments ago. That pale pink flesh. Unprotected. That had been his first reaction after the shock of seeing her naked, the flesh glowing in the half darkness of the bus. She had seemed so . . . he'd groped for the word, found it in the old language, tried to translate it into

English, and came up with only: unprotected. Or perhaps innocent. But innocence had vanished when she had turned and seen him staring at her. Anger instead. And her anger had stung him, as if he had been caught peeping at her, as if he had been one of those sleazy persons in Times Square who pay money to look at naked girls. He dreamed sometimes in the night of dusky girls, rounded and full, whose flesh flirted with his eyes through wisps of veils. He had never actually seen a woman or a girl without clothing, except for photos in magazines. Not until this girl, Kate. Her slim flat buttocks and the fullness of her thighs had startled him.

His face was still warm now as he looked at her. She was not yet aware of his presence, or if she were, she was pretending he had not entered the bus. One of the little boys waved to him. The boy with the missing tooth. Miro did not wave back. He would feel ridiculous waving to a child. Let the girl talk to them and wave to them. That was her job. The boy continued to seek Miro's attention. The girl looked up. Miro searched her face for signs of anger and found none. Worse, perhaps; she acted as if he was not there at all, was invisible or transparent. The child waved again and called out: "Hi." Brightly now, smiling for the first time. The girl said, "He likes you. Why don't you wave back?"

Miro was confused, his face warmer than ever, the pulse throbbing in his temple. He waved at the child, his hand strangely limp, and managed to croak: "Hello." He meant his voice to emerge strong and confident, but he was betrayed by his voice, which was suddenly too high and too false. His face now scarlet, Miro turned away from them, pulling the mask over his head. He looked out of the slit in the windshield pretending to study the scene outside. He was puzzled, bewildered, but a small place inside him was sweet with pleasure. The girl had spoken to him; she was not angry. And now he could recall the sight of her nakedness with pleasure, a stirring inside him that he had never known before.

Raymond was a good boy. He always did what his mother told him to do. He loved his mother. She was pretty and she always smelled nice. She bought him toys and games but she did not spoil him. His father spoiled him. Or tried to. He loved his father as much as he loved his mother but in a different way, of course. Sometimes, it puzzled Raymond. He liked to cuddle with his mother and nuzzle his face in her neck. But he liked to sit with his father, side by side in the chair. He would sit there quietly while his father watched the Red Sox on television. He liked the smell of his father, too. His mother smelled sweet, like perfume. His father smelled like the outdoors, like the shavings that fell when he sawed the fireplace wood.

Raymond's mother had gray hair and his father was bald. He heard them say: "Raymond is a late baby." He worried when he heard them tell people that. He knew what *late* meant. It meant not on time. It was not good for people to be late. "Come on, we're going to be late," his father would call to his mother when they were going out and the baby-sitter was there. "If we're late, there'll be hell to pay," his father said one time in the car when they were going somewhere. "Don't be late now," his mother would tell his father on the telephone. Raymond would lie awake at night, thinking of being late, thinking of going downtown with his mother and meeting people and hearing someone say: "But a late baby is such a pleasure." Raymond didn't know what a pleasure was but he knew what being late meant. He began to cry a lot. He began to get stomach aches. He tried to do things to make his mother and father proud of him. To make up for being late. He kept his room neat. He washed up good before eating. He did not fidget. He did not eat candy except at special times.

Now in the bus, Raymond did not fidget. He was afraid of the men in the masks. He was afraid they would find out he was a late baby. He was glad the girl who drove the bus sometimes was here. She reminded him of his mother even though her hair was not gray. Her name was Kate and he liked that name. She had told him that he might be able to help her. Like the times he helped his father carry in wood for the fireplace. People were glad when you helped them. He would help Kate.

Waiting to help her, he kept his eyes closed.

But not all the time.

He opened them sometimes.

First one, then the other.

Sometimes, both of them—but only a little bit so that no one would notice. Especially not the bad men. They would be angry because he did not eat the candy. And that would be just as bad as having them find out that he was a late baby.

Artkin summoned Miro at last.

Antibbe climbed aboard the bus and nodded his head toward the van. Antibbe seldom spoke, and when he did his voice was a hoarse growl as if speaking were painful to him.

"He wants you," Antibbe said. "I will watch the girl."

Miro glanced toward Kate, wondering what her reaction would be to this hulk of a man. Some men are menacing merely by their presence; Antibbe was one of these, and even more so in the mask. Miro considered that Antibbe could be a poet inside, gentle even, but outside he gave shivers. The thought surprised him: Where do thoughts like this come from? He never used to have thoughts like this, like wild birds flying. He had been content to let Artkin do the thinking, the planning, the pondering.

Kate was looking at Antibbe with apprehension. Or perhaps fear. It pleased Miro that the girl did not look at himself that way and seemed to relax in his presence. I am winning her confidence, he thought, as Artkin said to do.

"Be careful, the snipers," Antibbe growled as Miro pulled the mask over his head.

Miro said to Kate, "I will be back."

He turned abruptly away from the girl, afraid that his promise to return was a display of protection; he was certainly not here on the bus to protect her. He felt her eyes on him as he stepped down and out of the bus, onto the tracks. The van was only a few feet away but he had to be careful. He would have to crouch because of the snipers even though the guardrail was high enough to provide some protection. The space between the railroad ties made him conscious of the river far below. Miro did not trust the rotting wood, and this made him step gingerly toward the van.

The interior of the van was even hotter than the bus. It was smaller than the bus and cluttered. It smelled of something stale or gone bad, like food left out too long. Stroll stood at the back of the van, peering through the slit in the taped rear window. He did not turn as Miro entered. Stroll was always solitary, as if he were alone on the planet. Yet he was a beautiful driver and Miro loved to watch him steering the car.

Artkin stood before the CB monitor, his maimed hand twisting a dial. He greeted Miro with a nod of his head. The air suddenly came alive, a crackle of sound, static, and then a voice leaping from the monitor:

"KLC. Draw back at the angle. Then report on the zero-nine-six. Repeat: KLC. Draw back at the angle. Then report on the zero-nine-six."

Another voice: "Parallel. Parallel."

Then silence.

"They are using a special code of course," Artkin said, "but we have been supplied with it."

"What were they saying?" Miro asked. They had used monitors in other operations, although Miro had never paid much attention to what was being said. The messages were always in code, and Miro found codes tiresome. It was bad enough using the American language and trying to think in this language without having to learn codes as well.

"They are saying nothing we do not know," Artkin said. "Deploying their men, stationing them at strategic points. Mostly, they are using words to substitute for action. They, too, must wait."

Growing bolder, Miro asked, "And what are we waiting for?"

Stroll changed his posture at the back window. A slight movement, but eloquent because Stroll could remain motionless for hours. Perhaps I have surprised him by asking a question of Artkin, Miro thought, and he took pride in the matter. But hadn't Artkin said that he had treated Miro as a boy too long? And wouldn't he earn his manhood soon, if not today then tomorrow?

"All right, Miro. Tell me what you have seen from the bridge and then I will tell you what you have not seen."

"I see that we are surrounded. That the police and the soldiers are everywhere around the bridge. They have set up headquarters in the building across the ravine. Snipers are in the woods. Helicopters fly above us sometimes. We have the children on the bus. And the girl. One child died." He hesitated. Was there more? He was amazed again at Artkin, the way he had of turning his defense into an offense. He had said he would tell Miro everything and instead Miro was doing the telling.

"Good," Artkin said. "You have summed up the situation as far as your knowledge could do so. Now this is what you cannot see, Miro, what you cannot know." Artkin wiped some beads of perspiration from his forehead with his good hand. "We have entered an alliance. With people who are not of our nation. We are not the only revolutionaries, Miro. They exist in all nations, even here in America, this so-called democracy. I cannot tell you with whom we have made our alliance—even I do not know. Sedeete is in charge of that phase of the operation."

Sedeete. The use of the name filled Miro with awe. Sedette was above Artkin, above everyone. He was the planner and the mover. Miro had only seen him twice; once when he had ended his schooling and was about to depart for America. Sedeete had shaken the hand of each of them, in the old grasp of freedom fighters. A small man with burning eyes and lips like thin knives. His hand in Miro's had been curious: like old cardboard, dry, as if his skin had been replaced with false flesh. The second time had been a few days ago in Boston when Sedeete sat on a park bench with Artkin in the Public Gardens. Miro had remained in the van while Stroll and Antibbe stood watch at various points. Miro had only gotten a fleeing glimpse of Sedeete, afraid to look too long at him, as if Sedeete's glance could somehow poison him from afar. Sedeete was the leader of all the freedom units in North America. The realization that he was involved in the bus operation made Miro see how important it was.

"It is enough for you to know, Miro, that our strategy calls for us to hold the bus and the children until the demands are met," Artkin said.

Miro waited, hoping that Artkin would tell him the demands without making him ask.

"The demands are these, Miro. We seek the release of political prisoners held here in the States. We must show the world that revolutionaries cannot be held in jails. Second, we are demanding ten million dollars. This is to continue our fight, to finance our operations. Third, we are demanding that the Americans abolish a secret agency within their government. This is an agency that operates throughout the world. It is not our concern, Miro. Our concern is two things. The money, of course, which we need desperately, particularly American dollars. And the fact that we have been able to form an alliance and work with others."

"But why is an alliance important?" Miro asked. "Our work has gone well, Artkin. You said so yourself many times. The bombings, the explosions, they've made our presence known, they've made our cause public."

"Because, Miro," Artkin said, sighing patiently, "there must be a step beyond violence. Explosions and assassinations and confrontations cannot buy us back our homeland. They are only steps on the way, to call attention. After the terror must come the politics, the talking, the words. At the proper time, the words carry more power than bombs, Miro. So while we still use bombs, there comes a time when we must use words."

"Words," Miro said. He was tired of words. He had been trained for action, violence, and now he felt betrayed. Artkin had always said that every action they took was a statement, and now the rules were changing. He also realized that Artkin was not truly in command. Sedeete loomed in the background. They were like puppets here on the bridge, and Sedeete held the strings.

"Be patient," Artkin said. Perhaps he saw the doubt or the disillusion in Miro's eyes. "We are in a time of change. This alliance we have formed will be good for us in the end. Today we help them to destroy a secret agency, and tomorrow they will help us in another step to free our homeland. Our causes are different, but we can help each other. There will be many more bridges, Miro. This operation is only the first."

"What about this operation? What happens now? How long do we wait?" Miro felt like the girl asking these questions because she too had asked them of Artkin.

Again Stroll made a movement and again Miro wondered if he had asked one question too many.

"When the demands have been met, a special helicopter will land. We—you and Stroll and Antibbe and myself—will board it. We will be taken to the airport in Boston. From there, we will be flown in a jet across the Atlantic."

"To our homeland?" Miro asked, a sudden surge of hope lifting his spirits.

"Not yet, Miro. Home is a thousand alliances away. But they will fly us to safe territory where we can rest a while."

"But why should they let us go?"

"We shall take one of the children along on the helicopter. He will be our passport. Or perhaps it will be a girl child. I have not yet decided. One child is as good as sixteen or twenty-six."

"If one child is as good as sixteen, then why did we take the bus in the first place?" Miro asked, throwing caution aside, letting his anger carry his words.

"Miro, Miro, you have forgotten what you learned in the school. The *effect* of the operation is the reason for the operation. Simple escalation is the answer, Miro. Remember? One hostage in peril is effective, sixteen hostages in peril is sixteen times more effective, although the *life* of a single hostage—and in particular a child—is as effective as sixteen times the threat." Miro was always dazzled by this kind of arithmetic. "We seek the effect, Miro. We do not kill without the effect being the reason. Without the effect, there is nothing. So we took sixteen children as hostages for the effect, to capture attention. They do not seem to know it—yet how can they not know it?—but the media, the television and the radio and the newspapers, they are our allies. Without them none of this would be possible. A child held hostage in a secret place does not have the effect of sixteen children held hostage high on a bridge for all the world to see through the television, to hear through the radio, to read about in the newspapers."

Miro nodded. It made sense but it also fatigued him. At least Artkin was now confiding in him, explaining their position. He also had not taken offense at Miro's anger and impertinence. He had asked bold questions in the presence of Stroll, and Artkin had answered the questions.

"This is what happens now, Miro. Sedeete is the negotiator for the demands. The deadline for meeting the demands is nine o'clock tomorrow morning. If they are not met by that time, the children die. We, too, perhaps, although we have had that risk from the beginning of our operations here in the States. But Sedeete and those in our alliance are certain the demands will be met. Violence and blood pour out of American television, but these people do not really have strong stomachs. Up to now they have been spared the agonies of other nations, older nations. They will not allow the death of the children."

"How will we know when the demands are met?" Miro asked.

"The monitor here. The monitor has a special frequency developed with ingenuity. The fequency will allow a signal to be given to us by Sedeete. At six this afternoon, to tell us that the negotiations are in effect. At midnight tonight, to tell us that all is going well. At nine o'clock tomorrow morning, to tell us the demands are met. That is the deadline: nine tomorrow morning. Now, this is important. If we do not receive the signal at nine tomorrow, it means the operation has failed, that demands are not being met and I must take necessary steps. The first step: kill the children to show that the demands next time must be met. Then I must determine the best way to save ourselves, if possible. But, as you know, Miro, saving ourselves is not important. Except if we can live to fight again. Otherwise, to die in these circumstances is the best way to serve."

Miro felt that Artkin would never die. He accepted the possibility of his own death as a natural consequence of his work. But it was impossible for Artkin to die. They would never win the freedom of their homeland if men like Artkin died. The world would become meaningless without him. So would Miro's own life.

"Any more questions?" Artkin asked. Astonishingly, there was a teasing in Artkin's voice, and almost a smile on his lips. "I have found that you are good at questions."

Miro swelled with pride. His lungs were full of it as he drew a breath. He stood at attention without realizing he was doing so. To die with Artkin would be a great thing. He had pity for those who lived without dedication, like so many Americans his age he had seen, like the girl in the bus.

"Back to the bus now, Miro. Watch the girl and the children. Tell me when you think they need more of the drugs. And the girl, see that she is useful with the children. If she is not, then tell me and you can do your duty with her when you choose. But as long as she is useful to you, let her be."

"Yes," Miro said, still proud, proud to have been taken into Artkin's confidence, to have had his questions answered.

Stroll stirred again at the window. Let him stir, Miro thought, let him make comments with his stirring. Today, I am equal with him.

As he turned to leave the van, Artkin touched his shoulder in a man-to-man gesture. He wished that Aniel was here so that he could share this moment with him.

Kate was uneasy during the time that Miro was in the van. The man that Miro called Antibbe—*An-ti-bee*—stared at her relentlessly, his eyes following wherever she went, whatever she did. The eyes burned into her. They weren't the kind of eyes she'd ever seen before. They weren't filled with lust or longing, or with anything else for that matter. They were flat, dead eyes, as if they had no life at all except what they reflected, and they were now reflecting her. Her image caught, suspended in his eyes. Crazy thought, spooky.

To get away from those eyes, Kate walked among the slumbering children. She acknowledged how many times the children had offered her distraction during bad moments. On the other hand, she wouldn't be here if it weren't for the children. So one thing canceled out the other, didn't it? Yet, in a way, it was just as well that she was here instead of her uncle. He had no patience at all. He couldn't stand kids. He also had ulcers and high blood pressure. He had taken the part-time job of summer bus driver to supplement his retirement income from the Hallowell Plastics Novelty Company and, what the hell, he said, he only had to put up with the little bastards less than two hours a day. The rest of the time he either drove senior citizens around to shopping centers or took chartered groups to the beaches and seacoast resorts.

Kate sat down next to Monique. The child's nose was running. Kate dug into her pockets for a Kleenex but found only the bunched-up panties, a small damp ball now. Kate allowed the child to wipe her nose on her arm, although her stomach revolted at the act. Would her uncle do that? You can bet your ass he wouldn't. She noticed as the day wore on that she was swearing more. In her thoughts, anyway. Not exactly swearing but becoming gross in her language. She thought: Maybe there's a relationship between bravado and cowardice. And tough language made you feel tougher, braver. Maybe the tough kids at school, tough in behavior and language, were really the scared ones after all, the way she talked tough to herself now to keep up an appearance of bravery. Christ, she thought, surprised at the idea. And immediately felt better even as she pondered how the same word *Christ* could be both a curse and a prayer. And, crazy thought, did Christ know the difference when he heard his name called? Ridiculous, Kate told herself, as she wiped her arm on her jeans. Or am I getting hysterical? All these thoughts and that guy Antibbe staring at her from the front of the bus plus the key in her sneaker. The key that represented her hope for getting out of here. When Miro came back and the man Antibbe was gone, she would have to sit in the driver's seat and figure out how she could drive the bus with those tapes on the window. And Miro—what about him? And that look in his eyes? Could she make use of that?

Monique was dozing again, and Kate left her to check the other children. She slipped into the seat next to Raymond, wondering if he was actually sleeping now or only pretending. Feeling her presence, he opened one bright eye. Kate smiled at him and he closed the eye again. She took his hand in hers and held it. After a while, the hand went limp and his breathing became the rhythm of sleep. She hoped he could sleep the time away, like the other children. She wished she could sleep. Maybe she should have taken some of the chocolate and let herself lapse into sleep. She felt despondent suddenly, despite the knowledge of the secret key. She was not heroic, her life had not been a rehearsal for heroic deeds. She was trapped on this bus with the kids, in the hands of madmen. She'd seen them without their masks so they would never let her get away. She wriggled the key with her toes. So. So, what did she have to lose then? Why shouldn't she try a wild ride on the bus and try driving the damn thing out of here? Nothing to lose. No place to go but up. Why not go?

Hey, wait a minute, she thought, what's going on here? Why this great surge of hope when actually I'm down in the pits? Why not? Things couldn't possibly be worse, and once you accept that, you can begin to hope. You can begin to take chances, be reckless because, what the hell, you have nothing to lose, right? Right. She closed her eyes, exulting in the sudden flow of thoughts. Let's count the blessings, she thought, the things on Our Side. The key. Miro who was obviously the weak link among the hijackers. Little Raymond, even, who was bright and intelligent. And this new knowledge of hers, this new hope. She caught her breath, pondering a new thought: the possibility that hope comes out of hopelessness and that the opposite of things carry the seeds of birth—love out of hate, good out of evil. Didn't flowers grow out of dirt?

She let her breath out and felt her lips trembling. Christ, such a revelation. She wasn't certain now whether she was praying or thinking or what. She had never been a hotshot in the philosophy department, had never in fact been required to *think*, to go beyond what was written in textbooks, and thus the wonder of her thoughts and the new knowledge they had brought her filled her with a kind of ecstacy she had never known before. Not ecstacy of the emotions but of the mind, the intellect.

Overwhelmed, she looked around for someone to share it all with. There was no one, of course. She bent down and planted a kiss on Raymond's tender cheek. Softly so that she wouldn't wake him if he slept.

And then Miro was back.

"Why are you doing this?" she asked, trying to keep any harshness out of her voice, needing to seem friendly and interested. By *this* she meant the bus, the children, the hijacking, this entire nightmare.

Miro knew her meaning. "It's what we must do," he answered in his carefully measured English, as if he were walking a verbal tightrope. "Our work, our duty."

"You mean your work is to kidnap children, hurt people, terrorize them?" The hell with trying to appear docile, let the chips fall.

"It's the war. It's all a part of the war."

"I haven't heard of any war."

He looked so young, so defenseless, the brown eyes innocent, the mouth sensitive. So unlike the person in the mask.

After Antibbe left the bus with one last lingering look at her, Kate had retired to the back seat and sat there, pondering the time ahead and what she must do. One of the things was winning Miro over. Or at least getting him to talk, to let down his defenses. She had seen that look in his eye and had to take advantage of what that look meant. He had to look upon her as a human being. More than that: as a desirable young woman, and not a victim. She knew the perfect terrible truth of the situation: she had to make it hard for him to kill her. Thus, when he looked her way on his return as he checked the children, she forced a smile to her lips. A weak substitute of a smile maybe, but it had done the trick. After a few moments, Miro came and sat beside her on the back seat. He removed his mask and placed it on the seat beside him.

And now they were talking about some kind of war, something she hadn't expected when she'd started this conversation. But, she thought: At least, we're talking, we're communicating.

"The war is going on all the time," Miro continued. It was a topic he loved, a topic they had discussed much in the school. "Our duty is to let the people know the war exists, that the world is involved in it, that no one is free from war until our homeland is free." He wished Artkin was here to listen to him, to see how well he had learned his lessons.

"Where's your homeland?" Kate asked.

"My homeland is far from here. Across the ocean."

Kate detected a wistfulness in his voice. "What's its name?"

Miro hesitated. He had not said the word of his homeland for so long—like his own name—that he wondered how it would sound on his tongue. And he hesitated also because he did not know how much he should tell this girl. He wanted to win her confidence, but he must not betray himself or the others. If he did not say his name aloud to Artkin, how could he tell this girl the name of his homeland? "You do not know the place," Miro said. "But it is a place of beauty."

"Tell me about it," Kate said.

"I have never been there. I have never seen my homeland."

"You've never seen it?" Kate asked, incredulous. "How do you know your homeland is so beautiful then and worth all—all this?"

"I have heard the old men talking in the camps and they have said how beautiful it is. They say that if you take off your shoes, you can feel the richness of the land on the skin of your feet. The orange trees are fruitful and the flight of the turtle dove and the lark is balm to the eyes and spirit." He was quoting the old men now, and his voice was like music. "The river there is gentle and the sun is a blessing on the earth and turns the flesh golden. The sky is the blue of shells washed by fresh rains."

Kate thought: This strange, pathetic boy.

And then remembered that he carried a gun and one child had already died.

"Katie, Katie," one of the children cried.

The cry brought back the reality of the bus, the heat,

the oppressiveness, the plastic pail nearby that reeked of urine.

Kate listened, but the child did not cry out again.

"The old men in the camps," Kate said. "What camps?"

Miro was pleased with her question. She was becoming interested: he was doing his job well. But how could he tell her about the refugee camps, that endless string of filthy crowded places he and Aniel had drifted through in the early years of their lives, unknown and unwanted in a terrible kind of anonymity? They had existed on the generosity of strangers, and when they did not encounter generosity, they stole. Aniel was the expert at theft. Sometimes Miro acted as a decoy in the makeshift marketplaces, while Aniel's swift hands grabbed and clutched whatever was at hand. Nothing was ever useless. You made use of whatever came your way. Even the time Aniel had wrenched a battery from an old abandoned truck. They had bartered it for food. The food was spoiled and sickened them. But then the battery was also useless. How could he tell the girl all this?

"My people are outcasts, our homeland occupied by others. But we were allowed to live in camps," Miro said, wanting to hold her interest without telling her about the hunger and the stealing and the begging. He did not want to diminish himself in her eyes.

"You said *we*," Kate said. "Who was *we*? Your family, your parents?"

"Only my brother Aniel and me. He was two years older."

"How about your parents?"

He translated the American word *parents* into the word for mother and father in the old language and tried at the same time to summon feeling, emotion, *something*, but could not.

"I never knew my father," Miro said. "I never knew my mother." For some reason, he always felt guilty about this: not knowing his parents, having no remembrance of them. Why did he feel guilty? He pondered this in the small hours of the night when sleep did not come. Do not waste your time with the past, Artkin had told him once. The past is gone; the present is enough. And the future will bring us back our homeland. He had said to Artkin: "My father and my mother are in the past, and if I don't remember them, who will?" And Artkin had turned away without an answer. So Artkin did not know everything, after all.

Now, Miro said to the girl, "I have no memory of them."

There was a strange expression on her face. What was it? Sadness? No. He would have treated a sad look from her with contempt. He did not want her sadness. The look told of something else but he could not name it. A strangeness in her eyes as if in a moment she would either burst forth with laughter or dissolve in tears. He was confused. No one had ever looked at him with such—such intimacy before. And to cover his confusion, he found himself telling her:

"In those days, there were always attacks on the border. And there were times when we did not know who was enemy or friend. Mines were planted in the gardens. Cattle was slaughtered in border raids. Planes dropped bombs or raked the earth with machine-gun fire. Homes were burned. Aniel said that our father and mother were blown up by a mine planted in our garden. Someone told him this. But Aniel also said: 'Let us not talk about it. They are alive in us. As long as we are alive, one of us, then they will never be dead.' And now Aniel is dead."

"I'm sorry," she said. And he looked at her again. For signs of—he did not know what. She was only a girl, an American at that, and she meant nothing to him outside of the fact that she was his victim, his first death. She should have been dead hours ago. She would be dead hours from now. By his hand. His gun. Who was she to say *I'm sorry?* Only those most intimate should say words like that. Even Artkin had not said them, but had turned away in respect.

Kate sensed that she was losing him, that she had said something to turn him off. He had been so open one moment and then his faced had closed her out, his eyes dropping away. Maybe it hurt him to talk about his parents and his dead brother. Maybe her instincts were correct, after all, and she was on the right track: he was vulnerable, sensitive. She couldn't lose him now. Instinctively, she turned to the oldest weapon she knew, remembering how it had never failed her.

"You speak English beautifully," she said, flattering him, of course, but knowing there was truth in the flattery. "You must have a special talent for languages."

Miro blushed with pleasure. But like so many things, there was pain in the pleasure. The girl's statement also made him think again of Aniel. Poor Aniel. Dead before his time. Good with weapons as Miro had been good with languages. Aniel had been good with his hands as well. His hands, too, were weapons. He struck swiftly and with accuracy. He knew the parts of the body that were most vulnerable to attack. His hands could kill as quickly as a knife or bullet. But Aniel had been a slow student in other respects. Especially language. Miro had excelled at languages. You should have been a scholar, his instructor had once said. In a time of peace, he might have have been.

The girl persisted: "Did you go to a special language school?"

"I went to a special school," he said, wondering if she noticed the irony of his words. And then he found himself telling her about this special school that was not really a school at all, not with desks and chairs arranged neatly like the pictures he had seen of American classrooms. The building was sunk into the earth with no windows. The blackboards were sheets of wrinkled paper pinned to the walls. The education received in the school was intense and concentrated. You are here to learn what you must know to survive and what you must know to gain back our homeland, the instructor had said. He was an old man with many scars on his face. He taught the use of weapons and explosives. Combat: with the knife, the gun, the hands. The diagrams of the human body outlined on the blackboard were indelibly stamped on Miro's mind. Even now, Miro could touch certain spots on a body that would cause a victim to grovel with pain. Yet Miro had enjoyed the other lessons more: reading and the languages. The languages were important because everyone was trained for a destination, to carry out revolutionary acts throughout the world. The countries of Europe. Africa. America. Miro and Aniel were assigned the English language; their destination, America. The instruction actually concentrated only on the rudiments of language, enough to read street signs and order food in restaurants and stores so as not to call attention to themselves, to know what newspaper headlines meant or newscasts on radio and television. And the usual vocabulary of intimidation to be used in robberies, confrontations: *pigs, war, up with your hands, we will kill, die.* . . . Miro discovered that he had a talent for language, and a teacher who had lived in Brooklyn many years before (Miro felt a kind of regret when later they had blown up the post office there) had encouraged him and brought him books and gave him special instructions. But he had to study in secret. This had amused Aniel. The school itself was a secret place; while the authorities allowed the refugees to live citizenless in the camps, they forbade them to conduct schools, making education clandestine, carried out under guard. "Here you are," Aniel had said, "studying secretly in a secret place. A secret within a secret." And yet Miro knew that Aniel was proud of his brother's talent, just as Miro was proud of Aniel's skill with weapons.

"Katie, Katie," the child cried again—or perhaps it was another child—and Miro started in surprise. He had been carried away by his words and his memories, and had in fact forgotten the presence of the girl to whom he was addressing those words. Had he revealed too much of himself?

The child persisted in her cries.

"I should go to her," the girl said, apologetically.

Miro was pleased with her reluctance to leave. Perhaps she had been interested in what he had been saying. Perhaps he was winning her over, at last.

The crying child was Karen, the dark-haired girl who wore tiny onyx earrings, no larger than periods at the end of sentences. She was half asleep, whimpering, having a bad dream maybe. Kate drew her on her lap and pressed the child close. The child spoke unintelligibly, gibberish, the language of dreams and nightmares.

"There, there," Kate murmured, herself dreamy, held in the thrall of Miro's words. The boy stumbling through refugee camps, no parents, his brother dead, taught violence in an underground school. She thought of her own life, placid and pointless by comparison, safe and secure. On the edge of pity for the boy, she realized that their two lives had brought them here to the bus where she was a victim, not the boy. His life had prepared him for this moment. Hers hadn't. He was prepared to hurt and to kill. She was prepared for nothing. Certainly, not to be brave. But being brave shouldn't be something that you are trained for, should it? Bravery should be an interior quality, summoned from within. Where is mine? Kate asked herself dismally. Where is mine?

The child dozed, the dream having passed, her face serene once more. Although it was hot in the bus, Kate drew comfort from the child's closeness, the warmth and softness against her. She closed her eyes and it was nice to rest for a moment, suspend her thoughts, drift in the darkness.

She might have fallen asleep for a few moments, floating beautifully, suspended in time, cut loose from here and now. Then her eyes flew open and Miro was there, crouched on the floor beside her.

"Do you like Elvis Presley?" he asked, his face so close she could smell his breath, faintly acid.

The question was so unexpected that she laughed, laughter as unplanned as a hiccup.

"Why do you laugh?" He was serious, unsmiling.

"I'm sorry. I didn't mean to. You surprised me." Boy! Elvis Presley. "Yes, I like Elvis Presley." But she didn't, really; she neither liked nor disliked him: he was passé, old stuff, dead a few years now. "I didn't expect you even knew about Elvis Presley," she said.

"I have been here in America more than three years. I have a transistor but it is not allowed on operations. I like the Bee Gees, too. And disco."

He stood up abruptly and turned away, as if he had

said too much. Kate watched him return to the back of the bus. She marveled at him. He could tell her casually about his ability to hurt a person with his hands, but it embarrassed him to say he liked Presley and the Bee Gees.

After a while, she placed the child on the seat and made her way down the aisle. She had to continue her pursuit of Miro. She couldn't lose him.

He sat alert as usual; he never really relaxed, always watching, always on guard.

She sat in the seat next to the last, legs out in the aisle, conscious of the key in her sneaker. Keep him talking, she told herself, keep him talking.

"If you and your brother wandered through the camps with nobody to look after you, how did you end up in school?" she asked.

He said nothing. Didn't stir. As if she had not spoken.

She felt enclosed in the silence, removed from the small sounds of the children sleeping and stirring, sounds that had become so familiar that she was barely aware of them, like the sound of her own breathing. The outside world was distant, far away.

"Artkin," Miro said, finally. "Artkin found us in the camps and brought us to the school."

"How old were you?"

He hesitated again. Should he be telling the girl all this? He had never spoken of these things before. And his age. He was not sure, really, of his age. In the camp, they had given him a birth date, and it had been chosen to suit his height and weight and growth. The same with Aniel. So now he passed for sixteen but it was possible that he was fifteen or seventeen. "I was eight or nine when I went to the school," he said. "I do not remember." But he did remember how Artkin found them. They had been living for a few weeks in the ruins of a house that had been burned. The smell of embers filled their nostrils as they slept at night. It was the season of chill, when the winds blew dust across the land and the dust entered everywhere, even the pores. Aniel was older and a hotblood. So he let Miro make use of whatever they had to cover them, old coats and rags or sometimes paper. Artkin came along and saw them. They were afraid of him at first. He stared at them a long time from across the street one morning as they prepared for another day of foraging for food or whatever they could turn to food. Artkin crossed the street and questioned them gruffly. "Are you hungry?" he said finally after asking them about their comings and goings and receiving only vague answers. The answers were vague because they had only a dim idea of where they were and where they had wandered, and for how long. Wandering was their way of life and they did not question it—just as one does not question how one learns to run or walk or leap across puddles. When Artkin asked if they were hungry, they gave him a positive reply. He grunted and beckoned them to follow. He took them to the school in a nearby refugee camp. It looked like all the other camps from the outside, but Miro and Aniel learned that it was really a training school for freedom fighters. Artkin left them there. The camp and the school became their home for the next few years. Artkin visited them on occasion. He recruited other fighters, although Miro and Aniel were the youngest. Artkin seldom allowed an expression to show on his face, but he seemed proud of their accomplishments; interested, at least. Then at last their assignment was given: America. And their leader: Artkin.

Miro hesitated now. Again, he wondered: Have I told too much?

Kate, almost mesmerized by Miro's recital, asked, "What was your assignment in America?"

"To bomb," Miro said. "To plant bombs in the cities. Brooklyn, the post office. Detroit, the automobile plant. Los Angeles . . ."

Headlines leaped to Kate's mind. Television newscasts as well. Those bombings. The explosion in the Brooklyn post office where innocent people died—a young mother and child blown to bits as the woman mailed a letter. And the others. Kate was hazy about statistics, how many dead, how many injured. But she remembered that people had died and were hurt. She remembered the passing outrage she'd felt in the moment before the commercial came on or just before she turned to the entertainment section of the paper to see what was playing at Cinema 1 or 2 or 3 or 4. But for an agonizing moment she had been caught up in the horror of the news, and now that horror visited her again as she sat across from Miro and realized that he had been involved in all those explosions which killed and wounded innocent people. And mixed up with the horror was guilt, as well, for having allowed the terrible events to pass over her without impact except for that small pause of momentary sympathy before she checked on the movie she might go to that night.

"All those people who died," Kate said. "How could you?"

Miro looked at her patiently. "But this is war, Kate. I told you. We are at war, and people die in wartime."

She wanted to say: Don't call me Kate, don't you dare call me Kate. But didn't. Another small defeat.

"Didn't you feel anything for them at all?"

"Who?"

"Those who died. The mother and child in the post office. Didn't you realize what you were doing?"

Miro looked at her blankly. What did she want from him? What did she want him to say?

My God, Kate thought, turning away, looking at the blank taped window. She brought her knees up to her chin and sank back in the seat out of his view. She did not want to see him at this moment. He had seduced her with his pathetic tale of wandering through the camps as a child and had somehow enlisted her sympathy. But now she recognized him for what he was: a monster. And the greatest horror of all was that he did not know he was a monster. He had looked at her with innocent eyes as he told her of killing people. She'd always thought of innocence as something good, something to cherish. People mourned the death of innocence. Someone had written a theme paper on the topic in school. But innocence, she saw now, could also be evil. Monstrous.

Miro sat in anguish, empty of words now. Anguish because he could not understand this girl. And he also wondered why he tried to understand her. Her life was one way of living, his another. He felt anger as she continued to remain hidden from him, out of sight. She did not see the world as it existed. She looked at the world through her ignorant American eyes as she drifted through her schoolgirl years. His life had purpose and direction. Dedication. Who was this girl to turn away from that kind of dedication?

He came to his feet and looked down at her. She seemed shriveled into a ball, her face indistinct in the shadows. He searched for words to bring her out into the open again. "The blood that spills is the fuel that will bring us back our homeland," he said, trying to recall slogans he had learned in the school. "Some must die so that others may live. We are all soldiers although we wear no uniforms."

"But the children," Kate said. "They're not soldiers. What do they know about the world, your terrible war? One child has already died. He might have grown up to be somebody special. Someone who might have been a great man."

"Aniel, too, might have been a great man, but he is dead and you do not mourn him," Miro said. But even as he said the words he pondered a truth as bleak as the camps he had roamed as a child: Had he mourned not for Aniel but for himself?

part
7

Where are you, Ben?

I've been waiting here for you more than a half hour, although it seems longer. But you haven't appeared. I returned to the room after swallowing the pill and visiting awhile with Dean Albertson—he's as long-winded as ever, impossible to get away from—and arrived here to find the room empty.

This is a nice room, Ben, as rooms at Castle go. Your bed is neatly made—you have always been fastidious. Your papers are piled in a neat stack near the typewriter; a theme paper, I suppose. The walls are bare like your room at home. Clutter always irritated you. I lived in the John Quincy Adams wing as a student. On the second floor. I went up there today before going to meet Dean Albertson and stood outside the room. The door was closed, the corridor deserted.

But I didn't go in.

Maybe I was afraid of seeing ghosts.

Which is ridiculous, of course. If I should encounter ghosts here, they would be friendly ghosts. I spent some of the happiest years of my life here at Castle. Too brief, however. And too swift. Along came the war and I didn't see this place for years and years until they asked me to appear as a guest lecturer some time ago.

I was always happy here, Ben, with my friends. I hoped you would be, too. And make friends like mine. Jack Harkness was my closest friend. On the Monday morning after December 7, 1941, we joined up together, fled this place in a fever of patriotism, hitched a ride and made our way to Boston. We served overseas together. The Pacific Theater. The islands. All those places for which the streets at Fort Delta are named. I walk down Iwo Jima Avenue at Delta and remember Jack Harkness who died there and is buried there. I vowed over his grave that he would not have died in vain. Does that sound naive and embarrassingly patriotic and old-fashioned? A vow like that? We were poorly trained in those days, Ben, but trained superbly in one thing: patriotism. There are all kinds of patriotism; ours was pure and sweet and unquestioning. We were the good guys. Today, there is still patriotism, of course. But this generation is questioning. This generation looks at itself in a mirror as it performs its duties. And wonders: Who are the good guys? Is it possible we are the bad guys? They should never ask that question, Ben, or even contemplate it.

I am sorry, Ben. I apologize. For the preaching. Or maybe this is an apology for something else.

Trying to say now what I could not say to your face earlier.

Actually, I found it difficult to look you in the face, in the eyes, this morning. Not afraid of what I would see. But afraid of what you would see.

I see *Knights and Dayze* on the table there.
My old yearbook.
All those names and faces. Where are they now?

And where are you, Ben?

And when you return, Ben, what do I tell you?
What do I say?
Should I attempt to explain everything?
And where do I begin?
At the beginning. Where else?
And the beginning was last August, when the bus was on the bridge and the children held hostage and one child already dead . . .

We knew within hours, of course, with whom we were dealing: terrorists well practiced in their craft. Merciless. Fanatic. A nationwide investigation, swiftly organized and placed in action, told us what we needed to know and indicated what our course should be. We had learned by the experience of other nations about terroristic tactics and, to some extent, by our own experience. We also knew the line we had to follow: Don't give in. Bargain for the sake of stalling, buying time. But refuse to accede to the demands.

Meanwhile, there was activity the general public did not know about. One branch of our armed services had been training in counter-terrorist operations, prepared to move into situations when and if they occurred. A unit of this branch was dispatched to Hallowell and deployed itself in the woods surrounding the bus and the van. They brought the latest equipment, particularly a sophisticated version of the stun grenade. This grenade would be the key to the operation, particularly since children were involved.

We deduced that there were probably no more than four terrorists involved in the hijacking. A man named Artkin who was well known for terrorist activities and had been under surveillance for some time, suspected of participation in bombings in Brooklyn, Detroit, Chicago, and Los Angeles. Two others identified as likely participants were a man called Antibbe, who also used many other aliases, familiar to authorities in the Middle East and Europe as a mercenary, and a black named Stroll, known primarily as a technician, expert with explosives, machinery, etc. There was one other, whose identity was not known to us at that time. A person with no record. This person, as far as observations could be made, remained in the bus, obviously in charge of the children and the girl. The fact that he was an unknown entity and thus unpredictable in his actions—particularly where children were involved—gave us additional concern. Artkin, we knew, was capable of the most violent acts. His casual bombings had resulted in more than thirty deaths, six of them children.

Our major break came when we captured a man known as Sedeete, the acknowledged leader of certain terrorist groups in the United States and Canada. He could tell us nothing; he was critically wounded in the events surrounding his arrest. His capture left Artkin in command of the situation. This had both an advantage and disadvantage for us. The advantage: if we could convince him that Sedeete was captured and the operation aborted, he could bargain for his own freedom and release the children. The disadvantage: as a fanatic he could kill the children and die on the bridge as a sign to the world, and especially the United States, that his cause was worth dying for and that others were willing to kill and die for the cause.

Meanwhile, we were aware of a ploy that had become known to many in our occupation as the Messenger Gambit. We did not believe that the terrorist factions knew we were aware of this tactic. Thus we were in a position to use it to our advantage.

And that, Ben, brought us to you.

And brought you to the bridge.

And me here to this room where I pace the floor, waiting, wondering where you are, when you will return. And the most terrible thought of all: Will you return?

I just checked my watch. After one.

You've been gone a long time.

I left the room for a few minutes to see Dean Albertson. To inquire about you. To see if you had gotten in touch with him or his office. To inquire whether anyone had seen you about the grounds. I did not wish to raise an alarm and thus embarass you. He said he would make "discreet inquiries."

So I'm waiting.

The snow is falling again but softly. There's barely any wind and the flakes tumble to the earth like feathers.

There was always a good deal of snow here at Castleton. Fine ski country. I used to love to walk in the snow. On lonesome afternoons, I would set off by myself, head out toward Brimmler's Bridge because one needed a destination.

How much time I spent at Brimmler's Bridge.

I wonder: Do you go there, too?

If you don't come back soon—say, in another thirty minutes or so—perhaps I should search the grounds instead of merely waiting here. Perhaps you have been upset by my appearance here after all this time and fled the room, Castle, and are lost out in the woods, in the snow.

Thirty minutes.

The wind has risen now and the temperature has dropped. I have come in from outside and my hands are still raw and cold. The room is also cold. The heating system never worked that well here at Castleton.

I have talked to Dean Albertson again, but he dismisses my fears. He tells me not worry. The boys are in a holiday mood this weekend, he says. Some of them have gone off to Pompey. Others are out in the woods, some are ice fishing on Drake Pond. But I feel he doesn't realize the truth of the situation, how much we both went through last August on the bridge and afterward, and how my appearance here has possibly upset you. He suggested I take another tranquilizer. How does he know I take tranquilizers? Did he spot me swallowing one earlier? I had no time to question him because I was more concerned with you than with myself.

So I set off to search for you, to see if you were somewhere in the vicinity. I was surprised at how well I remembered the place. The years have not dimmed my memory of the grounds, the tortured paths through the woods or the gravel untarred roads leading to Pompey to the south or Barreston to the north. The snow obscured the footpaths, but I persisted. I resisted calling out your name. I was afraid that you'd hear me when you were with the other fellows and wouldn't want them to think your father had to go searching for you in the woods as if you were ten years old.

A group of fellows were ice fishing at Drake Pond, huddled around a spot in the center of the pond, the flames from a small fire spitting at the falling snow. They passed a bottle around and each took a swig from it. I crouched among bushes watching them, feeling like a spy. I remembered passing a bottle around like that years ago on this same pond. So there I was, spying on my own boyhood. I squinted but could not see you among them. The funny thing is that I could not see their faces; they were too far away for that. But I sensed that you were not with them. I would know you anywhere, Ben, without seeing your face. Would know the way you held yourself, the way you slanted your head when you listened closely or concentrated on something. I always thought that I knew you better than anyone else in the world, Ben. Better than I know your mother, in fact, although I have been more intimate with her, of course. But I have known you from the moment of your birth. I witnessed your growth, watched your progress, saw your transitions from baby to child to Little League ballplayer to adolescent. The school at Delta was monitored by the test and measurement procedures I instituted. Thus, I saw your growth both as a son and a student. I knew so much more about you, Ben, than you ever suspected. And loved you all the more. Knew your weaknesses and loved you for trying to overcome them because I knew that you could not exceed your limitations. Although you tried. Take your Little League baseball games, for instance. All the measurements showed us your potentialities, your susceptibility in stress situations, your vulnerabilities, to the point where it became possible for me to know how well you might or might not do in a game, in a given situation. Yet, I never subjected you to behavior intervention or modification, Ben. I did not want to subject you to the experience of those involved in Inner Delta. You were not an enlistee there or an enrollee, like the other men and women. You were my son; after all, you were not being trained to be sent into the field.

I regret, of course, my knowledge of you. I never found any satisfaction in the knowledge—how could I? Because I usually knew beforehand your reaction to situations, whether you were doomed to failure or not.

How I wish I had never known.

I have digressed.

I have allowed my thoughts to take me—and you—to places where we should have not gone, to all those tests and measurements. The important thing right now is finding you and confronting you face to face. And that brings me back to the search for you. I had a sense as I was walking along of also searching for myself, knowing that as my son you are heir to my own vulnerabilities. So I thought: Where could he be? Where could he have gone? And I remembered Brimmler's Bridge, the same bridge to which I went as a student, to sit and ponder life and its mysteries.

I set out for the bridge, fighting my way through the snow and the wind, the paths obscured, and no one in the area. The wind howled and the snow whirled viciously, blindingly. I was without gloves or scarf and plunged my hands into my coat pockets, but this made walking difficult. Finally, I had to expose my hands to the freezing air so that I could balance myself as I walked, reaching out for trees and bushes to help me on my way. I finally reached the bridge. It was deserted. The snow was so thick that I could not see the river below. I searched for your footprints but there were none. The new fallen snow would have obscured them, of course. There had been no guarantee that you had gone to the bridge. I was merely following my instincts. Putting myself in your place again. I looked hard and long into the snow. I told myself there was nothing else to see. There was no reason to see anything. Or could I see myself down there? Perhaps I should be the one to take that leap and never have to worry about you again and what I did by sending you to that bridge last summer. A voice inside me said: Why not? Why not jump? I listened, the wind howling around me, as if an actual voice were speaking, whispering to me, echoing in my blood, my bones.

I turned away, shivering in the cold, and came back here, certain that I would find you waiting for me.

But you were not here. Are not here.

It's as if you were never here.

There is no trace of you at all.

If you'd been out in the cold and the wet, certainly you would have tracked in snow or left puddles in your wake. There would have been the smell of wet clothing in the air. Or your wet jacket hanging from the hook in the corner.

But there is nothing.

And I'm afraid to look in the closet. Suppose I opened the door to the closet and found nothing in there, no clothes, no trace of you at all?

I found something else, though, in this room.

The pages, near the typewriter.

They weren't a school assignment or theme paper, after all.

Maybe I knew all the time what they were. Is it because I know you so well that I also know the words you would write?

And what you wrote tells me that you've been here and now you're gone.

They also tell me what I've done to you.

Oh, Ben.

Come back. Please come back. So that I can ask you to forgive me.

part
8

"What are you looking at?"

"Nothing."

"You have been looking out the window for a long time. Do you see something out there, Kate?"

She hated it when he called her Kate. "No, there's nothing out there. I'm just bored. Tired of this bus, tired of everything."

Which was true, of course, but not all of the truth. She was tired and exhausted and disgusted, but she was also determined. Determined to do something, to make use of the key, her only hope now. She knew she could not depend on Miro any longer or her foolish hopes of winning him over. You don't win monsters over. Even a sixteen-year-old monster. So she had to rely on herself.

Kate decided to take her chances with the bus. Her

new-found hope—*nothing more to lose*—was the only thing to cling to now. Peering through the slit in the rear window, Kate studied the bridge to see how far she had to drive the bus to get them out of here. There were obstacles, of course. She would have to drive in reverse. And she'd have to drive blindly. The tape would prevent any vision through the windows. She'd have to start the bus and put it immediately into reverse, holding the wheel steady as they bounced over the railroad ties. If she lost control, they could plunge to the river below. Her eyes surveyed the parapet. Solid, cast iron probably, sturdy. If she went off course, the parapet looked strong enough to prevent the bus from crashing off the bridge.

She sighed, blowing a damp strand of hair from her cheek. How far would she have to drive the bus? She tried to measure the distance. She was lousy at this sort of thing. Artkin had said the bridge was the length of a football field—one of *your* fields, he had said—and the bus was halfway across. It would be like one of Ron Stanley's touchdown runs. Not so far as that. If Ron Stanley could do it with a football, certainly she could do it with a bus. The thought, ridiculous as it was, cheered her.

She left the rear window to check the front of the bus, the driver's seat, the instrument panel. The aisle had become strewn with the children's small debris: pieces of chocolate-stained Kleenex, discarded lunch bags and wax paper, gum wrappers, paper napkins. You're a lousy housekeeper, Kate, she told herself. As she scooped up the debris, she felt lighthearted for the first time in—how long? Ages, it seemed. Her decision to drive the bus out of here one way or another had lifted her spirits, restored her balance, even if it didn't work out. Miro approached her, holding out the plastic pail for her to drop the rubbish into. She did so without looking at him. She wanted nothing more to do with him.

Squinting through the narrow opening in the windshield, she saw the rear-view mirror on the top of the left front fender. It was at least one foot high and probably a half-foot wide, providing a good view of the tracks behind the bus. But she wouldn't be able to see the mirror when she sat behind the wheel. The damn tape would block the view. There was a simple solution: she'd merely rip the tape from the window after starting the motor.

She sat behind the wheel now, resting her hands on it. This would be the biggest worry—the bus itself, starting the motor. Would the engine start quickly enough? The bus wasn't exactly new; she had no idea of its age. The transmission was sluggish and stubborn, the gears difficult to shift. Yet all she'd have to do was shift to reverse and leave it there. Another thing in her favor: all buses used to transport children were inspected by the state and were supposed to be in good running condition.

She felt Miro's eyes on her but ignored him. He didn't know about the key. He probably figured she was just bored, restless. Let him look as she rehearsed what she must do. Place the key in the lock. Push the clutch pedal down to the floor. Shift from neutral to reverse. Rip the tape from the window. And Miro: he was a factor in her plans. She would have to wait until he took one of his periodic trips outside, when he stood just outside the door of the bus to get a breath of air.

She inspected the tape on the windshield, saw one or two places where the tape had loosened near the window's edges. She could easily pull the tape away and give herself a clear view through the windshield. She would also have a view of the van, which faced the bus. And whoever was in the van—Artkin or the other two—would be able to see what she was doing if they looked through their own slitted tape. But she'd have to take that chance.

One question remained. *Could* she take that chance? Could she actually try to drive to the bus out of here? Could she ever be that brave? She could rehearse in her mind all the things she had to do to get the bus moving. But she wished there were a way she could rehearse her bravery.

He watched the girl.

As he had never watched anyone before.

From all over the bus, from many angles.

Was "watch" the proper word? In the past, at Artkin's command, he had watched doorways for someone to appear, watched cars, watched airport entrances.

But this watching was different.

It was watching but also looking.

It was using his eyes as a blind man would use his hands.

Like now:

Kneeling down to give the appearance of adjusting the buckle on his boot, he squinted up at her, seeing the right side of her face only as she bent over one of the children. An errant shaft of light outlined her profile. He would love to trace that delicate profile with his finger, down her forehead, over the nose that had a slight rising in it, and across the lips to the delicate chin. He pictured her, foolish thought, opening her mouth and nibbling at his finger. The thought startled him. Where do such thoughts come from? His finger in her mouth, her lips nibbling? He straightened the buckle, stood up, and moved away.

Later, he watched without seeming to watch as she arched her back wearily, lifted her head and raised her face to the ceiling of the bus. She massaged her shoulders, then her back. She looked as if she were taking a shower, the water invisible as it splashed her body. She looked like a bow, poised for the arrow to be shot. She thrust her arms behind her, as if they were wings and she could fly out of here. The movement caused her breasts to press forward, straining against her jersey. He had always been embarrassed by the sexual displays of American girls. They were without shame in their boldness. But Kate was not being bold now. She did not know he was watching. His eyes were half closed as he sprawled in the seat, pretending indifference. Kate was only seeking to relax, to ease her tired body, as if she were alone in her room. He could not take his eyes away from her breasts. They were not large but they stood out prominently. He wondered what it would be like to hold one of her breasts in the palm of his hand as if it were a small puppy to be petted and caressed.

Still later, Kate was at the back of the bus again, looking out of the window. Miro noted the way her blond hair flowed down below her shoulders. The small of her back sloped gently toward her buttocks. What word did the Americans use? Ass. A blunt coarse word. But he could not deny the attractiveness of the rounded buttocks in the tight jeans. He tried to recall her buttocks as he had seen them in that earlier glimpse, unclothed, uncovered, pale and pink in their roundness, the glimpse too swift, too little. Now Miro was able to study her buttocks without hurry, for she seemed preoccupied with whatever view lay beyond the window. He should be suspicious, of course, and he would be if it were anyone but an American schoolgirl, one of those hollow, empty-faced girls without any purpose in life. They were beautiful the way flowers were beautiful, with no purpose except to be beautiful. He continued to stare at Kate's body while Kate continued to look out the window. Let her look. She was like a flower and flowers should be allowed to follow their inclinations. Until the season ended and they died.

She knew he was watching her, that look in his eyes again, and she was both exhilarated and appalled. A while ago, he had looked at her with hard, cold eyes and talked of death and destruction, and she'd had no doubt that he could kill her or any of the children without hesitation, without conscience. And then she'd felt his eyes upon her, following her, drinking her in as if she could quench some terrible thirst of his. She thought of all the talk about feminism and equal rights and realized it melted away when it came to certain things. Like that look of his. She hadn't been flattered by that look, by his interest. In fact, she resisted his attention, pretending not to notice, not wanting him to know that *she* knew, not wanting to respond. Yet a small dim hope flowered within her again. Was she foolish to let it flower? Her emotions were on a seesaw now: up, down, up, down.

She looked up now to catch Miro turning away, averting his eyes quickly. But not in time. She knew, though, that she could not rely on him and what he had seen in her. She had to rely on the key. And that unknown quantity: herself.

The long afternoon burned on, the heat increasing, pounding at the taped windows, pressing on the roof of the bus like a giant's hot hand. The helicopters came and went, roaring and throbbing and fluttering and then receding, fading away; and after a while, Kate discerned a pattern in their arrivals and departures. Every fifteen minutes. Occasionally, a siren howled, piercing the air with its sound of emergency: something gone wrong, something gone askew. Distant shouts sometimes reached them, and Kate would press eager eyes to the window slits but would see no movement out there, no activity, the woods shrouded and still. Yet, the helicopters and sirens were reminders that someone was out there, someone was watching. But what could they do as long as the hijackers held the children?

Artkin visited the bus on occasion, consulting with Miro, checking the windows, glancing at the children and at her with indifferent eyes as if he were taking inventory in a store or warehouse, checking numbers, quantities, nothing else. He fed the children more doped candy and Kate protested only feebly, knowing her resistance was useless. Once, Artkin offered her the candy, holding out a piece of chocolate.

"Why not sleep, like the children?" he said, that gentleness in his voice she did not trust anymore. She saw him whirling Kevin McMann above his head.

She shook her head.

"The time will pass more quickly," he said.

She was almost tempted. But shook her head again. "No."

He looked beyond her, and Kate turned to see what he had spotted. Raymond's eyes were open, watching them. Those bright eyes.

"Hello, young man," Artkin said, going to the child. "You look wide awake. Haven't you been sleeping?"

Raymond flashed a look at Kate.

"Would you like some candy?"

Raymond looked at Kate again, questioning her with his eyes. Artkin caught the look.

"Take the candy," Artkin said.

Raymond's chin began to tremble.

"What's your name, boy?"

"Raymond," he said, the name a whisper. His eyes were agonized as he confronted Artkin.

Oh, Raymond, Kate thought. You poor kid. Take the candy, eat it, don't try to be brave, sleep this whole nightmare away. She knew that it had been futile anyway to count on a five-year-old child for help. Futile and foolish. But he had been a forlorn hope at a time when she had needed hope, no matter how forlorn.

"Don't you like candy, Raymond?" Artkin asked, that deceptive gentleness in his voice again, a voice that would haunt her dreams.

"My mother says it's not good for my teeth," Raymond said bravely in his old man's voice.

"But this is a special occasion, Raymond," Artkin said. "You can wash your teeth good when you go home and you won't have any cavities from the candy."

Again, Raymond looked at her.

Kate said: "Take the candy, Raymond."

Raymond's eyes filled with tears as he held out his hand to Artkin, palm up. Was he crying because he didn't want to eat the candy or because Kate had let him down, capitulated, sided with the bad guys? She had to make an effort to hold back her own tears.

"Now eat," Artkin said. "It tastes good, you'll like it."

Raymond put the candy in his mouth, chewed, the tears rolling down his cheeks, looking at neither Artkin or Kate.

"That's good," Artkin said. "And now, another."

Kate turned away.

Later, Raymond slept along with the children. She'd waited until Artkin left before going to him but he was already drugged, head lolling, jaw loose and slack. Had

Artkin increased the dosage? The other children also slept. Perhaps the drug accumulated in their bodies, didn't wear off but remained there. In the past hour or two, they had become even more docile, as if in a stupor. The drug also seemed to immobolize their bodies; since that first experience with the pail this morning, none of the children had asked for its use again. They didn't ask for food, either. Kate herself felt drugged. Her blouse was damp. Her hair hung in moist strands as if she hadn't washed it in weeks. The heat clung to her flesh, seemed to penetrate her pores, dulling her senses. Raymond's hand was in hers. She pressed it and Raymond pressed back faintly. Her legs felt heavy, as if huge weights rested on them, as if she had been running a long long time. She felt her head nodding, her eyelids drooping, and was too exhausted to resist the sweet lassitude invading her body so tenderly, so beautifully. She fell asleep, a deep dreamless sleep of clinging darkness. No bus, no children, no hijackers, no helicopters, no sirens. Nothing.

Miro watched her sleeping. She was like one of the children. Unguarded, unprotected.

If they went to Times Square again, he would ask Artkin to arrange for one of the girls.

He was curious.

Small beads of perspiration glistened on Kate's lips, like a moist mustache. A lock of hair had fallen away, revealing her temple, the cluster of small blue veins. The bullet in her temple would flower into blood.

He was sorry the bus driver had not been a man, after all. He would have been spared meeting this girl and seeing the horror in her eyes when she looked at him. She had said: Don't you feel anything?

What was there to feel? Miro wondered. A man lived his life and performed his duty and did what was necessary to survive. As Artkin did. How he wished he could be like Artkin someday.

Miro frowned as he looked down at the girl.

She stirred, lifted a hand to her cheek.

Miro moved away, in case she should awaken and see him there, like one who peeks at women.

Monique dreamed that Classie was with her. Sitting on her lap and hiding. Both of them hiding from everybody. Mommy, Daddy, Claire. Claire who was in the third grade and came home and didn't want to play with her.

In her dream, Classie was sitting on her lap but then she got up. All by herself. Classie was walking. Classie never did that before. She wasn't supposed to walk. But she was walking now. And then she was running.

She was running down the middle of the bus and the big man was running, too, with his big boots and he was going to step on Classie. Crush her. Kill her.

She wanted her daddy to stop the man.

She wanted her mommy to stop him, too.

But they were gone. Gone with Claire to school, and when they got home, they wouldn't want to play with her and they would let the man's boots step on Classie and crush her.

She screamed for Classie.

Look out, Classie, look out.

The man's boot was like a giant's boot coming down on Classie as she ran. But now Classie wasn't running. She was moving her legs but staying in the same place.

And here comes the boot.

She screamed again, the scream like a big fire coming out of her mouth.

Kate woke up and knew instantly, blindingly, where she was: on the bus, with the children and the hijackers. She kept her eyes closed for a moment more, reluctant to open them, to take up the burden of being on the bus again. The echo of a fading cry lingered in her ears. She opened her eyes. Were the children all right? She heard their soft snores, their heavy breathing. She looked around. They were all lost in the drugged sleep.

She moved her foot and felt the key cuddled in her toes. If she was going to try to drive the bus out of here, she'd better do it before it was dark, before night came on.

The moment was here then. But she didn't know whether she was ready or not. She had to summon a Kate Forrester she'd never known before: the brave Kate Forrester.

The steering wheel was in her hands and she was poised for action: one foot resting on the clutch pedal, the other ready to push down on the accelerator. She had rehearsed the steps she must undertake. In sequence. She had sat here for almost an hour, waiting. Going over the whole thing in her mind. But it was all futile, would go for nothing without Miro. The dash to freedom depended on him. He had to be outside the bus, standing at the doorway, so that she could close the door and shut him out. But Miro was showing no inclination to step outside, although he had done so regularly earlier. Now he lingered in the back of the bus, squinting out the windows. Once in a while, he walked among the children, checking them out, as if the children might be plotting among themselves, for heaven's sake.

Meanwhile, Kate was concerned about the failing daylight. Twilight had arrived delicately, like soot being sprinkled throughout the bus. Outside, light still lingered, that eerie time of day that was like dawn in reverse, the sky pale but growing darker, the sharp edges of everything growing blurred and indistinct. Peering through the slit in the windshield, Kate saw that the roof of the van was melting into the gathering darkness. If she waited much longer, she would have to use the headlights. The lights would shine directly into the van, causing an immediate alarm. She'd also been pondering another worry: What about the cops and soldiers in the woods? What would they do when they saw the bus moving? Would they fire? Would they figure that someone was trying a getaway from the hijackers or would they think that the hijackers themselves were attempting to get away or trying a diversion? She didn't know. She only knew that she had to take that chance. She felt certain they wouldn't shoot at the bus knowing the children were in there. She would have to gamble that they'd hold their fire, that they were under orders not to do anything that would further endanger the children.

The children, thank God, were still under the influence of the drugs, sleeping mostly, stirring occasionally, calling out once in a while. She was grateful for their drugged state at the moment, allowing her to concentrate on her plan. She felt an urgency to get going, to put the plan into action before she got cold feet or thought of something that would dash cold water on the plan. But she couldn't do anything at all while Miro was on the bus. She could only fidget here at the wheel and wait. And wait.

"It's hot in here," she called out now to Miro.

He took his eyes from the rear window and looked in her direction.

Once before she had complained of the heat and he had only shrugged.

Now, Kate grew bolder: "Couldn't you open the door for a while? It's stifling in here."

Miro came forward and Kate felt transparent, wondering if he were suspicious. Did he suspect she had a plot going? How could he unless he was a mind reader?

Miro kept his eyes averted from Kate as he stepped down to the door. He used his key to unlock the door. Kate then manipulated the lever that swung the two sections of the door open, allowing a small rush of air to enter.

"Isn't that better?" Kate asked, her voice sounding too sharp, too shrill to her ears.

Miro did not answer. He looked out the doorway. Kate sucked in her breath. Her hands were loose on the wheel, ready for the sequence of events that must take place as soon as he stepped outside.

But he didn't.

Suddenly, he squatted down and sat on the bottom step, his legs dangling outside, blocking any possibility of closing the door.

Damn it.

"Katie, Katie," a child cried out.

Damn it. She couldn't abandon the driver's seat, not after having cajoled Miro into opening the door. This was probably her last chance.

"Katie . . ." A child calling.

She didn't know who was calling her. They all

sounded the same when they cried out, emerging from the drugged sleep, stunned, reeling out of oblivion into the reality of the bus.

"I'll be there in a minute," she called back.

Miro stood up and looked toward the children.

"Be quiet," he said.

His command brought silence.

He looked kindly at Kate. "The children. They never leave you alone."

He remained standing there. Kate dared not move, felt as though she were standing on a tightrope. She smiled at him, what she knew must be a sickly smile, forced, strained.

He didn't sit down. Stood there, craning his neck. Then miraculously, he stepped down. And out. Less than a foot away but outside the bus. His back to her.

Kate heard her own sharp intake of breath.

Now.

She reached down and took the key out of her sneaker, having already unloosened the shoestring. She checked to see if Miro had observed her: he was still facing away from her. Kate placed her hand on the door lever. And hesitated. She wondered whether she should shut the door and then start the motor. Or vice versa. Suppose she closed the door and the motor didn't start? Miro would have time to sound an alarm. But suppose she started the motor without closing the door? He was only a foot or two away and could easily jump back into the bus. Her carefully planned sequence of events was disrupted, like jackstones spilling to the ground.

I'm no good at this kind of stuff, she thought. I'm not heroic, not brave. She glanced backward at the children. Maybe she was risking their lives unnecessarily.

For Christ's sake, Kate, come on, she urged herself.

Do it if you're going to do it. Don't do so much thinking. Do it.

She slipped the key into the ignition slot. The key lodged itself with a satisfying click. She then did several things at once. Pushed down on the clutch pedal. Released the handbrake. Placed her right foot in position at the accelerator. Blew an errant lock of hair out of her vision.

She managed a swift glance at Miro: still outside, still a step or two away.

Now.

She eased the gear shift into reverse, carefully, delicately because sometimes it made a noise. Not this time, though; it locked into place quietly. She didn't have to worry about more shifting. She was going to move in one direction only: reverse.

She turned the key in the ignition and pressed down on the accelerator. The engine moaned, a lazy reluctant sound: like a yawn. And like a yawn, sleepy, languid. Jesus. She pumped the accelerator, aware of a movement now at the corner of her eye: Miro. She swiveled the lever that controlled the door. The door closed with a gratifying swish. She turned to confirm its closing—and saw Miro's face, grotesque in the mask as usual but almost a caricature, his eyes and mouth forming ovals of astonishment. He might have been screaming at her; she didn't know.

She didn't know because the engine had come alive, pulsing and purring, sounding eager and confident, the way a motor sounds on a rainy night. She'd often thought of the bus as an animal, a plodding beast, elephant or rhinoceros. But the bus now sounded like a panther, a tiger, sleek, smooth. Or was she getting hysterical?

She jammed down the accelerator and let up the clutch, slowly, agonizingly, not wanting to stall the engine, conscious of Miro at the periphery of her vision and aware, too, that the children were stirring. But concentrating on the delicate balance of her feet on the accelerator and the clutch.

The bus lurched.

My God, the tape.

She ripped at the loose edge of the tape on the window and it came away like a Band-Aid from dry flesh. She pulled at another strip and another, uncovering the driver's side of the windshield, letting the strands of tape dangle from the right side. She only needed enough clear windshield to see the rear-view mirror perched on the fender. And now she could see it: where she had to drive. She could also see the van, its own windshield taped except for a narrow strip in the middle of the window.

Miro's shouts were audible now and he was pounding on the door. The children were calling out. The hell with being too cautious about stalling. She pushed down on the accelerator, jamming it to the floor. And she eased up on the clutch pedal. The motor raced, throbbing magnificently, its vibrations singing through her body, the bus itself shaking in response. Lurching again, the bus began to move backward, responding, not the sleek big cat anymore but a plodding beast—but moving, moving. Kate glanced at the rear-view mirror. She had to be certain the bus was on course. She adjusted the wheel. Let's go.

The bus jerked backward in a shuddering leap. Kate darted a glance at the door: Miro was trotting alongside. The bus was bouncing over the railroad ties in a jolting burst of movement. The children began crying. One of them fell with a thump to the floor. Kate continued to hold the accelerator to the floor.

Sirens sounded from somewhere. She saw Artkin erupt from the van, propelled awkwardly onto the tracks, off balance, like a skater out of control, careening wildly. Antibbe followed him, tripped as he emerged from the van, his huge body crashing to the tracks, his gun squirting from his hand like a bar of soap.

The bus gained momentum. Grinding, roaring, jouncing. Kate gripped the steering wheel tightly, holding on frantically as the bus staggered backward, the motor magnificent now in its power. She urged the bus on, pumping the accelerator. Miro continued to pound at the door. She could not see Artkin, but Antibbe had gotten to his feet and scrambled now toward the bus, moving fast for such a huge man. She saw, horrified, that he had jumped on the bumper and was now trying to get onto the hood, one leg seeking purchase there, the gun aimed directly at Kate. Would he fire at her point-blank to stop the bus?

"Kate!"

Miro's voice reached her, a scream, an animal in the scream. His hand was prying between the accordion pleats of the door as he ran alongside the bus. Antibbe was now on the hood, on his hands and knees, balancing precariously, the gun somehow still pointing at her. The kids were crying, screaming. What about herself? Was she screaming, too?

She poured all the strength at her command into keeping the accelerator against the floor—and the bus stalled.

Whined and fell silent.

Stopped without warning as if it had crashed against a brick wall.

Kate pitched forward and had to clutch the wheel tightly to avoid hitting the windshield. Antibbe was flung helplessly from the hood, the gun in his hand like a wand waved by a mad conductor. The children's screams seemed to rise an octave. She looked back at them. They had tumbled around the bus like loose change in a pocket.

Kate saw with dismay that the van was only thirty or forty yards away, not far at all, not far enough. She thought she had driven farther than that, might have almost made it to the end of the bridge. Slumping in the driver's seat, she lowered her head. She was close to tears, tears of frustration and anger. Anger at her own ineptitude. Damn it. She had failed. Failed utterly, failed the children and herself, missed her best—maybe *only*—chance of escaping, getting out of here. Had done nothing but make things worse. May have brought on retaliation, doomed them all.

And she was oozing down there.

Her migraine returned.

These things she hated about herself.

Miro pounded at the door, each blow like a nail into her flesh.

Without looking up, she swung the lever that admitted Miro into the bus.

For a split second, she thought: This is it, I am going to die. She closed her eyes, waiting. Then she opened them again, the darkness somehow worse than Artkin's fury: darkness too much like death itself.

Artkin's eyes were flat and cold and black. The mask emphasized their coldness, their mercilessness. Anger would have been better. Instead, this cold fury was directed at her, the eyes of a snake measuring the distance the fangs must travel to strike. She was also conscious for the first time of Artkin's teeth. The thick sensuous lips had hidden them before, but now his teeth were bared. They were discolored, gray, uneven.

He had ignored her until this moment of confrontation. When the bus stopped, he had gone to Antibbe's aid, helping the huge man hobble across the tracks to the van. Kate waited for sniper bullets, but none were fired. Miro stood at the doorway of the bus in answer to Artkin's command: "Watch her. If she moves, kill her," the words like doors slamming. Kate held on to the steering wheel for dear life. The children called to her, but she didn't answer. Not daring to move. The innocence of the children's voices filled her with sadness. More than sadness. Far beyond. She had let them down, betrayed them.

She felt Miro's presence at the doorway. Only once since the abortive escape attempt had she looked at him. And he had turned away, refusing to meet her eyes. She knew that he was now her true enemy. She had drawn the line between them.

Within a few minutes, Artkin returned to the bus, darting swiftly from one vehicle to another, crouched, wary. And still no sniper fire. He handed Miro a wrinkled paper bag. "Give it to the children. This is the last one," he said.

He turned to Kate.

"Stand," he commanded.

She rose to her feet and stood tentatively near the doorway. Artkin turned the key in the ignition and drove the bus to its former position near the van. The motor ran smoothly and, as if to mock her, did not stall. Artkin slipped the key into his pocket. Standing up, he faced her.

"Do not move," he said.

His hands reached out and gripped her shoulders. Hard. His touch repelled her. His hands began to move down both sides of her body, probing, inquiring.

"Turn out your pockets."

She turned them out, removing her wallet and the pathetic, bunched-up panties. Artkin slipped the wallet into his pocket. He unfolded the panties and shook them out. Was he expecting still another key to be hidden somewhere?

She became aware of the children's voices. In protest now. And Miro's voice, answering the protests. "Take the candy, take it." She heard one of the children retching, and another crying out, "I don't want any more." And still another: "I don't feel good."

Artkin ignored the developing clamour as his hands moved relentlessly across her body, over her stomach, down her thighs, his mained hand obscene, causing her to shudder. Up her legs, across her buttocks, impersonal, businesslike, the impersonality somehow more threatening and scarier than if his hands lingered, caressed, acknowledged that this was a woman's body he was searching. His hands moved up again, reached into her armpits, scuttled across her breasts. Her breasts might have been objects on a shelf.

"Your shoes," Artkin said.

She removed her sneakers. He looked into them, shook them and dropped them to the floor. She bent down, put them back on, left them untied. She stood again and realized that since that first cold look into her eyes, Artkin had not looked directly at her. He had avoided her eyes. And this was worse than his fury. She's heard that jurors, bringing in a guilty verdict, were unable to look into the eyes of the accused. It's difficult to look into the eyes of someone you will be responsible for killing. Miro had turned away from her. And Artkin averted his eyes. If she didn't feel so exhausted, so bankrupt, so utterly spent, she'd be dissolving in panic.

Now the children's cries were louder. Just as they'd been docile together as if taking the cue from each other, now they were protesting in unison, complaining of stomach aches, crying for their mothers, calling to Kate. She hazarded a glance toward them. Miro was holding out the bag of candy helplessly, uncertain how to proceed. One of the children, blond little Karen, leaned out of her seat, retching, on the verge of vomiting. Kate resisted an impulse to run to the child, to find the pail, to let the child get all the dope out of her system, to hold her while it all came up.

"Quiet," Miro yelled at them. "Be quiet."

But the clamour continued, wails and cries and moans.

"That was a serious mistake, miss," Artkin said, his face a breath away from her face. "It was a foolish mistake. Foolish because we are in negotiations now and your delivery is almost complete. Your stupidity might have ruined everything, touched off an attack."

She did not say anything. But a small hope flowered within her. If he was talking to her, giving her hell, then he probably wouldn't kill her. Not now, not yet.

"You are still useful to us, to a certain extent. Because of the children. They are getting the last of the drugs." He glanced in their direction. "And they are also upset now. You must take care of them, keep them quiet. We are in a delicate time with the negotiations. There must be no upsets. We are pledged to kill a child if the people out there take any kind of action. But they are also watching us, to see what might happen."

Hope was blossoming now. Time. She was getting

more time. Little Karen was still retching, huge gasps surprising from such a small child.

"One of the children is sick. Let me go to her," Kate said.

"No more tricks, miss. One more trick and you die. Believe me, this mission is worth more than your life."

"No more tricks," Kate promised.

Artkin stepped aside. Kate rushed to the nauseated child, arriving in time for the child to vomit all over the floor of the bus, a pinkish sickening fluid that splashed on Kate's hands and jeans, causing Kate herself to get sick to her stomach, even while she held the gasping, miserable child close to her and murmured whatever words of consolation she could muster.

"Miro."

Artkin's voice was flat, cold, deadly.

Miro hesitated, then stepped past the pool of vomit on his way to the front of the bus. Kate was able to squeeze out a small measure of compassion for him. Miro was about to get a bit of his own hell, and Kate knew she was to blame.

He felt the lash of Artkin's words. The sting.

He was afraid the girl could hear them, which would cause even greater humiliation and embarrassment.

But although Artkin's words were harsh, he spoke in whispers, furious whispers, full of anger, but whispers at least. And the children were still fussing, still crying, still seeking the girl's attention.

Miro was hardly aware of the background noise, however, because Artkin's words flayed him. He shriveled inside his clothes, his face was flooded with shame inside the mask. He wished he could cover his eyes, to escape Artkin's anger.

You neglected your duty. You turned your back on the girl.

165

You did not win her confidence. You almost wrecked this operation.

Miro winced, grimaced, glad that Antibbe and Stroll were in the van and were not witnesses. And yet it was Artkin who mattered, Artkin whom he did not wish to disappoint, Artkin whose praise he'd always sought.

I accept mistakes because humans make mistakes. And the young are expected to make mistakes. But to be careless is different. To be outside the bus with the girl inside, that was more than a mistake.

Artkin had scolded him before. But always with understanding. As a teacher scolds a pupil. But this was worse than a teacher reprimanding a student. Much worse. He was rebuking him as he would rebuke any other fighter, any other soldier. And Miro was plunged into despair. He had gained manhood on this operation. Artkin had confided in him. Treated him as a man. And he had failed Artkin. He had had no time to know pride in his manhood before he had made a mockery of it.

"One thing has saved you," Artkin said.

Miro did not move, did not breathe, tried in fact to even stop his blood moving in his veins. What? he wondered and dared not ask.

"I myself should have searched the girl. Or asked you to search," Artkin said. "I, too, was careless. I share the blame."

A sharing with Artkin? Even of guilt? Could this, too, be a source of pride? Or did it curdle pride?

And then Artkin told him to be on guard, more alert than before. "Learn by your mistakes," he said, a warning in his voice. "We are entering a crucial stage now. Stay on guard."

It wasn't until Artkin had returned to the van that certain words echoed in Miro's mind. Artkin had said:

One thing has saved you.

And Miro wondered miserably: Saved me from what?

Night penetrated the bus without Kate being aware of it, the mysterious border between dusk and night dissolved by the darkness. Actually, night only deepened the dimness of the bus, and yet it brought with it a kind of weariness that settled on its occupants like a comforting blanket. The air of the bus was stained with smells: urine (maybe my own, Kate thought dismally) and sweat and vomit. But somehow they seemed less pungent in the darkness, a trick of the senses maybe. Because the bus had been so dim throughout the day, Kate's eyes quickly became accustomed to the night's darkness. The children, with only one or two exceptions, responded gratefully to the arrival of night, falling into what seemed now to be a more natural slumber, breathing regularly, sleeping comfortably without the fits and starts and sudden harsh awakenings of the drugged sleep. One or two had vomited, gushing into the plastic pail, and some had complained of stomachaches. But Kate had been able to soothe their complaints, promising them that tomorrow things would be better, they'd be back home again with their mothers and fathers. The heat was still oppressive, no place for it to escape with the doors and windows closed. Kate felt she could bear the heat or anything else. The fact that she was alive, had survived the futile attempt to escape without any retaliation by Artkin against her or the children, made her feel that she could withstand anything, heat or cold, hunger or thirst. She realized that she'd hardly eaten all day long, except for small bites from the children's sandwiches. Her stomach now revolted at the thought of food. As far as thirst was concerned, she could put up with it, put up with anything.

Delicately, so as not to disturb little Karen who slept beside her, curled up on the seat, Kate raised herself to look out the window through the narrow untaped slit. Across the ravine, the windows of the pavilion were squares of yellow light. A bluish light flickered inside. The woods were quiet, suspended in the dark. No moon, no stars. A stand of birches gleamed like pale bones. She couldn't understand why nobody had fired when she started to drive the bus from the bridge. Was Artkin telling the truth? Were negotiations really going on? Would this mean their freedom was at hand?

Kate turned from the window. But not my freedom, she thought. She glanced toward Miro, who was sitting at the back of the bus, a black hulk in the night. She had heard Artkin giving him hell, blaming him for Kate's attempt to escape. She hadn't been able to understand Artkin's words, but the sibilant whispers left no doubt in her mind about what Artkin was saying. Later, as he passed by, Miro had looked at her with such malevolence, such hate, that she had clutched the child to her chest.

She sat down again, her limbs aching, all her muscles tight, cramped. At the same time, she felt dull, her head heavy, her eyes raw and itching. If she could only sleep, get some rest, escape from this terrible place for a few moments. Yet she knew that she had to resist sleep. Sleep was like a little death, and death was probably nearer than she knew. She wanted to remain alert and awake—and alive—as long as she could.

Miro brooded in the darkness, watching and waiting. On his guard. Watching for any movement at all.

Watching for whatever the girl might do next. She was bunched up with a child, sleeping perhaps. Perhaps not. Miro was unhappy. And puzzled. Puzzled because this was all new to him, being unhappy. He had never given much thought to his emotions. He was aware that other people were happy or sad. Those were the two emotions he had observed. Happy, unhappy. Like labels on a piece of luggage.

Yet, he himself was unhappy now. He was sitting in this bus with the children and an American girl and he had put a label on himself. He had never required a label before. During all the operations with Artkin, he had not thought about being happy or sad or even being afraid. He had concentrated on the operation and had known a kind of pleasure in doing well. That was all. But now he looked inside himself and knew a feeling he could only call sadness. The girl had asked: Don't you feel anything?

Confused by the thoughts, Miro stood up to inspect the bus. He did not want to risk another mistake. The girl Kate was more intelligent, craftier than he had suspected. Artkin had said: Never trust your enemies, no matter how docile they appear to be. And he had almost trusted the girl, had let down his guard because he thought she was docile, helpless. Had he diminished his guard against the girl for other reasons? He thought of her unclothed flesh and moved through the darkness to escape the thoughts.

The girl was apparently asleep, her blond hair like a small glow in the dark. She was the source of his trouble. She had been his first target and had eluded him. She had weakened him with her soft talk, her questions, and had made him talk too much and made him become careless. Padding softly to the door, he checked the lock. On his way back, he made certain the tape was still secure on the windows, the plastic still in place. He was careful not to wake the girl or the children. The children were a constant drain on his nerves.

He sat himself down rigidly on the back seat. He listened to the breathing and the gentle snoring of the children and the girl. Let her sleep. Tomorrow, the operation would end and he would have an opportunity to win back Artkin's favor. The children would be released and he would hold the gun to the girl's temple and then they would get away from this place.

He stayed awake through the night, humming to himself a Presley song. Just as he had trained his body to contain itself when there were no bathrooms, so had he trained himself to do without sleep when it was necessary, to remain awake and alert, his body on guard, his mind sharp and aware, his eyes able to penetrate the darkness and pick out any movement that might contain danger.

And that is why the girl's voice made him leap as it reached him from the darkness, close to his ear. "I'm sorry," the voice said, like a ghost in the night. He turned to the voice and realized with dismay that he had been betrayed again, this time by his body, which had fallen asleep even as he watched.

"Are you awake?" the voice said.

"Yes," he answered.

"I just wanted to say I'm sorry. For the trouble I caused you."

"It does not matter," he said, feeling again the humiliation he had known when Artkin rebuked him. Suppose Artkin had seen him leap here in the dark when the girl woke him? He hated her for this, and he had never hated before, not even the enemy. "I made a mistake. We learn by our mistakes."

"And what did you learn?" she asked, whispering, her voice hanging in the night as if apart from her body.

"To be on guard, always. To trust no one. Not even myself."

"That's sad," she said.

He could see her now, the spill of hair, the gleam of flesh. "Why is it sad? And why should it have meaning for you? We are nothing to each other." His voice was harsh beside hers, as he meant it to be. Yet he had never heard her speak so gently.

"It's sad not to trust anyone," she said. And even as she said the words, she was proving the truth of what he had learned. Because she was still using him, of course.

She had awakened a few moments ago to the stark knowledge that these hours of the night were her final chance. She knew she couldn't possibly escape tomorrow. Even if they freed the children, they could not afford to let her go. She had read doom in Artkin's eyes from the beginning. And now the boy hated her. He'd been blamed for her attempted escape and probably wouldn't hesitate to kill her himself.

Yet, she had reached him earlier. He had watched her the way a thousand boys had watched her. And he was her only hope. The others were animals. Not even animals, but robots. Merciless, heartless, they would not hesitate to kill anyone. Artkin's hands had moved over her body as if she were a mannequin in a store window. But Miro? That longing in his eyes. Could she make it reappear? Not in any hope that he would help her escape—that was impossible now—but to have him regard her as a human being again, someone whose life was precious, someone who'd stirred him a little, aroused him a bit, so that he might just hesitate, think twice, when a showdown came. She didn't have the key anymore and she didn't have Raymond, although

Raymond had been only a fragile hope. But she had herself. And trying was better than sitting here in the dark, doing nothing.

So she'd crept stealthily down the aisle, crouched and on tiptoe, not wanting to disturb the children. When she spoke to Miro, not planning what she was going to say, he answered immediately, his body jumping slightly. His voice was cold, hate made vocal, as cold and as flat as Artkin's voice could be when he was angry. It might have been the same voice, in fact; they might have been brothers or father and son. And when she told him that it was sad not to trust anyone in the world, she felt cheap and soiled and treacherous, knowing she was using the words to awaken him to her, using them the way she imagined a prostitute used her body to arouse a man.

"Haven't you ever trusted anyone in your life, Miro?" she asked. Had she ever used his name before?

"My name is not Miro," he said, the words a surprise to him.

"What is your name?" she asked, quickly, sensing that she had slipped through his guard again.

"I cannot tell you," he said, angry at himself for another betrayal. "Why should it mean anything to you? Why do you come to me like this in the night?"

"Because we're both human. We're both human beings caught in this terrible thing."

"I am not caught," he said. "It's my wish to be here. This is my work, my duty. There is no other place in the world for me to be at this moment but here."

She said nothing for a moment. She was really sad for him, the way it's possible to feel for something you do not understand. He was still a monster, of course. But who had made him a monster? This world, his world. Who was guilty, then: the monster or the world that created it?

"All I wanted to do," Kate said, "was say that I'm sorry I got you into trouble. You've been kind to the children and me."

She reached out her hand and touched his arm, hoping that her touch would convey the message she intended.

Her fingers on his arm startled him, her hand like a pale flower in the dark, her touch rippling his flesh like the breeze that moves the surface of a pond, his flesh now shivering in the same way. No one had ever touched him so intimately before. He held himself still, letting the quiver of her touch echo through his body.

And then she was gone, moving into the night and away from him.

Miro heard someone fumbling with the lock and came instantly awake. He blinked his eyes to see clearer, into far corners. Night and darkness still clutched the interior of the bus but the shapes of things were familiar to him. The unfamiliar would be a danger.

He made his way to the door, checking the children as he did so. They were asleep. So was the girl. He lingered near her for a moment. He touched the spot on his arm where she had touched him, her fingers as soft as flower petals. He turned away at the thought.

At the door Antibbe waited. "He wants to see you," Antibbe grunted.

Miro nodded. Action at last?

The van was hot, oppressive like the bus. Artkin's face

was pale in the harsh light of a portable lantern. But his eyes as usual were bright and alert. Stroll, as always, was shrouded in silence, watchful at the window.

"We have made contact," Artkin said. "The police, the soldiers, they are making offers."

"Are they willing to accept our demands?" Miro asked, envisioning the arrival of the helicopter and the flight across the ocean away from this country he could not understand.

"There are—complications," Artkin said.

"What kind of complications?" Miro asked, sensing trouble in the air, the way the wind turns before a storm.

"They say Sedeete has been captured."

Miro saw the doubt in Artkin's eyes and was not sure what the doubt was.

"Can we trust what they say?" Miro asked.

"That is the problem, Miro. There is no trust on either side—how can there be? But there is this: we did not receive our midnight signal from Sedeete, which shows they may be telling us the truth. Yet, it's understandable that Sedeete might have missed sending the signal for many reasons."

"The next signal is at nine this morning?

"Yes. If we do not receive that signal, then we know something is wrong."

Miro waited. A hundred questions crowded his mind but he did not want to voice them. Artkin was in command, and Miro sensed that he knew what he must do.

"The police and the soldiers have been broadcasting to us. They say that the operation is destroyed, that Sedeete and the others they picked up told them everything. They say we must free the children, that it will go easy for us if we do so. They have determined that the child who died was perhaps a victim of an overdose of drugs."

Miro felt as though the van, the bridge, the earth were crumbling at his feet. They had never been in touch with the enemy like this before. They had struck fast and quick and made their escape. Now they were surrounded and other people were telling them what they must do.

"We still have the children," Miro said, his voice sounding small in his ears.

"You have touched the crucial spot," Artkin said. "They can talk all the want, but the children are the most important thing."

"What do we do?" Miro ventured.

"The most important of all is to wait for nine o'clock when the next signal is expected. If it does not come, then I follow the original orders. Determine the best way to handle the situation, whether it involves killing the children or not. We must show them that we are adamant, however; that we will die here on the bridge with the children if we must. If we falter, we hurt our cause everywhere."

"We wait, then?"

"I have asked for proof of Sedeete's capture. But this is a stalling tactic. They can dig up proof in many ways. What we really need is information from them. We have to know how long they are willing to wait us out, whether they think we will really kill the children."

"But how can we find this out?" Miro asked. He was growing tired of talk and plans and possibilities. He ached for action.

"I have a plan, a method we have used before."

Stroll stirred, his movement signifying approval of whatever plan Artkin had in mind.

The monitor crackled, spitting static into the air. The

code words followed, meaningless utterances to Miro. And then a voice came through, crisp and clear. Artkin held up his hand for silence although no one in the van had spoken.

"We are seeking vocal contact with occupants of the van. We are seeking vocal contact with occupants of the van. Come in, please. Come in, please."

The voice was impersonal, as if it issued from a machine and not a person. The phrasing was measured, a recitation, like words read from paper.

"We hear you," Artkin said.

"We have the proof you requested. Directly from Sedeete. His watch, his wallet." Pause. "Repeat: We have the proof you requested. Directly from Sedeete. His watch, his wallet."

"You do not have to repeat," Artkin said, insolence in his voice, an insolence that cheered Miro. Artkin would bow to no one. "This may or may not be his wallet, may or may not be his watch. Having a man's possessions does not mean you possess the man." Artkin paused. "What of Sedeete himself? Let me speak with him."

"Impossible," the robot voice said. "He is hospitalized. In Boston. Unconscious. A bullet lodged in his spine."

Artkin showed no reaction. "I must have more proof, more than a wallet or watch."

"Tell us what. Repeat: Tell us what."

Artkin's head was bowed, in an attitude of thought. Miro found it difficult to breathe the heavy air.

"You said earlier that you seized Sedeete in Boston. At his room there."

"Correct. Positive." The flat, toneless voice.

"Then bring me something from that room."

"The room has been searched. And is now sealed." A long pause. "What is it you wish from the room?"

"Sedeete was hiding something in his room. Something special. If you get that something special and show it to me, deliver it to me here on the bridge, then I will believe you and we can begin to bargain."

Miro pressed his lips together in disappointment. He hated that word "bargain."

"What is this object?"

"In the cabinet of the kitchen, above the sink, you will find it. In a teacup there. Look in the teacup. You will find a round, gray stone. A souvenir from our homeland. Bring that here and then we will bargain."

Static burst from the monitor as if impatient to end the conversation.

"It will take an hour or so to get to Boston and another hour to return. But wait." The voice broke off and then returned. "We will radio Boston and have someone bring out the stone. Allow us an hour, ninety minutes perhaps."

"I will wait," Artkin said. He turned to Miro, a smile of triumph on his face, his eyes bright and flashing, his flesh flushed with youth.

Another voice filled the air, a contrast to the first voice: gentle, worried, human.

"Are the children all right? The girl?"

"Yes. They are sleeping. They want to go to their homes. But that is up to you."

"We don't want anything to happen to them," the human voice said. Miro wondered: Could this be the girl's father? Unlikely, of course.

"Neither do we," Artkin said. "But if something happens, it will be on your heads not ours."

Artkin flicked a switch and the monitor whined and then fell into silence.

"Is this good for us?" Miro asked, sensing that Artkin was pleased.

"As good as can be expected. When things go wrong,

we must use whatever we can, whatever we have at our command. The important thing now is time. We must wait until nine o'clock to see if we receive a signal from Sedeete or someone else. We must also wait for the stone."

"Is the stone important?"

Artkin smiled, looking at Stroll, as if he and Stroll shared a secret. "Yes, the stone is important. It buys us the time it will take to deliver it here. This stone has been used before in our operations. A stone from our homeland: it serves a purpose. You notice, Miro, that I used the word *deliver*. The stone must be delivered to us, here on the bridge. So it buys us more than time. It buys us a person who must bring the stone. And that person, whether he knows it or not, brings us information."

Miro was pleased that Artkin was pleased, although he found it difficult to follow these plans, these operations. All he knew was that there would be action when the nine o'clock deadline came and went. Action, a decision, instead of all this waiting, all this talk.

"We will take one step at a time. First, the stone. Then, we shall see."

Buoyed by Artkin's enthusiasm, Miro returned to the bus in good spirits. The night was still dark as he darted to the bus but there was the smell of morning in the air, a freshening in the darkness. And a freshening, too, in Miro's heart.

It happened moments later.

Antibbe had stepped aside to let Miro enter the bus. "All is quiet," he said, standing huge beside Miro.

Miro nodded. He was glad to be back on the bus. He had a sense of ownership. He had never felt responsible for something before, other than himself.

Antibbe left without speaking further, and Miro

secured the lock. Miro saw a flash of light outside the door: Antibbe's lantern. Somehow, Antibbe's lantern had gone on, illuminating him in its light, catching him as if in a spotlight's glare. Miro was surprised: Antibbe was slow and plodding but careful; perhaps he had touched the switch accidentally as he walked.

Caught in the sudden light, in the space between the van and the bus, Antibbe stood transfixed like a puppet pinned to a black wall. His eyes and mouth seemed to leap out of the mask and hang by themselves in the air.

Suddenly, he was lifted into the air a foot or so, then jerked backward as if by an unseen lariat. For a split second, he hung in the air, suspended above the tracks, crucified on an invisible cross, and then his body shuddered convulsively, his arms and legs twitching uncontrollably. The lantern fell from his hand but continued to shine on him where it fell. Blood gushed from the faucet that had been his mouth a moment before. The blood spilled across his chest like scarlet vomit. His eyes were wild in the mask, bursting from their sockets. And then he was flung backward, slammed into the darkness beyond him, swallowed up in the night.

It was only then that Miro heard the echo of the rifle shot.

The sound of the rifle had not been loud enough to awaken the girl or the children, but suddenly they were awake, as if Antibbe's blood had splashed like cold water on their faces. And, immediately, the woods and the building across the ravine and the bridge itself came alive. Spotlights flashed on, bathing the bridge in harsh brilliance. The trees rustled and vibrated as if occupied by a thousand waking birds. Sirens howled and Miro looked across the chasm to see a military jeep speeding away from the building. The building itself was suddenly swarming with activity, its windows lit up, men coming and going, blue lights blinking within. Miro saw Artkin at the doorway of the van, one foot on the railroad track, the other foot inside the vehicle. He stared at Antibbe's body as if studying it for future reference, as if he were memorizing its every shape and contour.

The children cried out, but Miro did not respond. He felt the presence of the girl nearby but did not turn his head. Then she was next to him. He heard her intake of breath when she spotted Antibbe's body in the spotlight's glare. Miro looked at her. There was horror in her eyes. As she turned toward him, Miro saw something else darting in her eyes, a small flash of—what? Triumph. He knew what she was thinking: One of them is dead, only three left. But Miro continued to hold her eyes until the deeper truth penetrated: the meaning of Antibbe's death as far as the girl and the children were concerned. An eye for an eye. The old words fresh as ever, fresh as Antibbe's blood. The truth dawned in the girl's eyes. Her jaw dropped, like a small trapdoor suddenly sprung. She reached her hand to that mouth. "Oh, no," she cried.

Miro had no more time for her. He turned again to see what Artkin would do now. But Artkin had reentered the van. A siren began to howl. Like a call to arms. Our arms, Miro thought. Action. At last.

Miro looked at Antibbe's body, which lay like a sprawl of rubbish across the tracks. Thank you, Antibbe, he whispered to himself in the same way he sometimes sang Elvis Presley's songs with no one else to hear.

That look in Artkin's eyes.
Miro knew that look. A calm look, serene. A look of

wisdom, as if Artkin had searched deep within himself and then arrived at a conclusion. He had seen that look when Artkin had finally declared, after nine hours under siege in the hotel lobby in Detroit: "We leave. Now." As if invisible gods were whispering in his ears, guiding him, lending him the wisdom of the ages.

As soon as Artkin stepped into the bus, Miro knew what the look meant and a shiver raised hairs on his flesh. Now it begins, Miro thought.

Artkin locked the door behind him. He crouched on the steps, beckoning Miro to him at the same time. Miro knelt above, his head inclined, eager to listen.

"They say that the shooting of Antibbe was a mistake. An unauthorized act. They were on the monitor right away and they said a sniper pulled the trigger by accident. A sniper who was too alert, too keen, his nerves strained and taut from watching in the night, too well-trained, so that his finger squeezed the trigger automatically when Antibbe's light went on."

The fools, Miro thought, to give such an excuse.

"It happens that way," Artkin said. "Reflex action. The way a hand is drawn from a flame before the brain has time to record the pain."

"You believe them?" Miro asked, incredulous.

"I believe them," Artkin said. "They have too much to lose at this point to risk such a thing. They have Sedeete. We have also selected a messenger to bring the stone. The son of one of their generals. We are on the edge of action."

Action, Miro thought bitterly. Their action, not ours. We sit here waiting while they take action.

Artkin looked toward the girl and the children. "They begged us not to take vengeance against the children, to put aside reprisals. But I told them that this was impossible. A child must die for Antibbe. Otherwise, they would have no respect for our cause, our position here. And they could kill us, one by one."

Miro, too, looked in the direction of the girl and the children. Which child? It made no difference to him.

Artkin's flashlight sent a feeble finger of light through the bus, touching the children's faces, remaining for a second longer on this one or that one. Morning had arrived but darkness still mingled with the tentative daylight seeping through the slits in the tapes. Kate blinked into the flashlight's beam as Artkin approached. She reached protectively for Monique and drew her near. This can't be happening, of course. What can't be happening? She could not allow herself to say the words, to form her thoughts into words.

Artkin snapped off the flashlight when he reached her. He was a wraith in the wan light, unreal, surreal. He looked around, studying the children. The children, in turn, looked at him with dull eyes. Some still slept. Those who were awake seemed to be drifting even while sitting still, as if the bus were a boat drifting aimlessly, taking them with it. Kate sensed their lassitude, was grateful for it. It was just as well that they didn't realize what was happening. What *was* happening? Nothing. It had to be nothing.

She looked up at Artkin. She had somehow reached the boy Miro. Could she reach Artkin? He looked at her with empty pitiless eyes. Then the eyes rested on Monique. No, Kate thought, pressing the girl to her, trying to absorb her into her own being.

Artkin bent over Kate.

"The boy," he said. "What was his name?

"What boy?"

"The boy who did not eat the candy at first. The little fat boy."

Kate tried to protest. Tried to say: Oh, no. But the words were strangled somewhere inside of her and the sound that came from her lips was a sound she had never heard before, as if she had suddenly found a new vocabulary, a new language, a language of despair and futility.

"His name." Artkin's voice crackled in her ear.

She couldn't say his name. Wouldn't say it. Maybe she could save him this way. Hide his identity so that Artkin couldn't find him.

But Artkin was moving away from her, the flashlight on again, sweeping the faces of the children.

"Ah, little boy. There you are. What's your name?"

"Raymond."

"No," Kate said. Meaning to scream the word but it limped from her mouth. She gathered herself to cry out: "You can't."

"Come, Raymond, we are going to leave this bus. And take a little walk. Aren't you getting tired of this bus, Raymond? You've been here a long time."

"Are we going home?"

Kate heard the little old man's voice and closed her eyes.

"Soon. You will be going home soon. First, let us get out of this bus. It's morning outside. The air is fresh."

Artkin's gentle, awful voice.

Kate felt something brushing her leg. She opened her eyes. Raymond stood there looking at her, his face bloated and weary.

"The man wants me to go outside with him. Is it all right?" he asked. His lips trembled. "I want to go home."

No. This couldn't happen. She couldn't let it happen. She thrust herself to her feet, stood to confront Artkin. "No," she said. "You can't do this."

"Miro," Artkin said.

And Miro was quick, leaping toward the girl, grabbing her, pinning her in his arms, pulling her against his body, smelling her sweat and the dim perfume that still clung to her body after all this time.

"Please," she said, struggling.

Artkin's face was close to hers. "You are only going to make it harder for the child, miss. If you continue this way, he will wonder why you are protesting, he will wonder what will happen to him if he comes with me. Let it be quick for him, miss."

Artkin led the boy down the center of the bus, speaking gently to him, promising him candy and lollipops and chocolate bars and kisses from his mother. The other children looked on indifferently, remote, as if from a far distance.

Kate pulled furiously against Miro, straining to break his hold. "Wait," she cried.

Something, the desperation in her voice maybe, made Artkin pause.

"Take me instead. Me, not him."

Artkin looked back at her over his shoulder.

"That's right—me. Instead of him."

And even while saying it wanting to deny it, deny the words. Christ, she wanted to live, to get out of here, to survive this nightmare. She didn't want to die here on this bus, this bridge, this morning, today. She wanted to live. But she cried out anyway: "Take me. Let Raymond go."

Artkin held her eyes with his eyes. She strained against Miro again, but he held her fast and firm.

"It must be a child, miss," Artkin said, as if apologizing.

Kate thought: How close I came. And shuddered. And hated herself.

Miro felt her sag in his arms and feared she had fainted. But he bent to peer at her and saw her eyelids fluttering.

Artkin picked up the boy to help him down the steps of the bus to the outside. Raymond looked over Artkin's shoulder at Kate, said something that Kate didn't hear, and then he was gone, the ghost of his bright, intelligent eyes and old man's voice lingering behind.

Miro felt her body loosen, as if her bones had suddenly come apart, rattling inside her body, disconnected, askew. He wanted to say something to soothe her spirit, to comfort her sorrow. But he could think of nothing to say. And then he thought: Why should I want to say such a thing to her? In war, a soldier does not bring comfort to his enemy.

Later, they heard the single shot.

Kate could not believe that it was the sound of a gun firing. Because that would mean that Raymond was dead. It had to be something else. Not a gun. But what else could it be? A door slamming? No, not out here in the middle of the woods, not a door slamming. But it couldn't be a gun either. Raymond mustn't die. Then what could it be? It had to be something else. But what? A car backfiring? Maybe. Anything. Anything but a gun. Something else. It had to be something else. A firecracker? Like the Fourth of July? How about that? A firecracker! No, not a firecracker and not a car backfiring but not a gun either. It has to something else. A gun means that Raymond is dead so it can't be a gun. It has to be something else. Yes, but if it isn't a car backfiring or a firecracker or a door slamming, then what could it be? What else could it be? Something. Something else.

All right. Fine. Something else, not a gun.

But what else?

Something, something else.
Yes, yes. But what else?
Nothing. Nothing else.
It was a gun and Raymond is dead.

part
9

Now I can see, Ben, that you are not lost out in the woods somewhere. Not lost at all, but hiding.

I have notified Dean Albertson of the situation, and he has dispatched Castle's security police to Brimmler's Bridge. To intercept you if you show up there. But I know that you will return here first. Before you do anything drastic. You said so in those pages near the typewriter. You said you would not make your pilgrimage to Brimmler's Bridge until you saw me again. You said you would honor your father. I know you will. Don't I know you better than anyone else in the world? Better than I know myself perhaps?

I am remaining calm, even though I acknowledge the contents of those pages you wrote and saw what I did to you. I have not even taken a blood-pressure pill, which, as you may have suspected, is not really a blood-pressure pill but a tranquilizer of sorts.

Should I have become involved in your life, Ben?
Did I even want to?
I was involved because you were my son, of course, and every father is involved with a son to a certain extent, some more, some less. Ours was more because we lived in the close confines of Delta. Your classes were monitored to provide data for my continuing studies on behavioral syndromes.

The taping of the telephone at our home was necessary because of Inner Delta. Monitoring has always been a vital part of operations. Messages to and from our home, instructions to be relayed or received, all of them had to be recorded. So we recorded all calls and filed them. The tapes were seldom referred to except for occasional checks. It was during those occasional checks that I heard your calls, to your friends. To that girl, Nettie. I was not an eavesdropper, Ben. I did not intend to invade your privacy. But I heard the heartbreak in your voice when she treated you so cruelly. And I ached for you, remembering my own heartbreaks at that age: a girl whose face I can barely remember now, although the ache lingers.

So you see how it was with you and me, Ben? I knew you as a father knows any son, and I also knew you as a student because the reports of your education were made daily to me. And I also knew the private side that a father seldom learns about, your relationship with friends like Jackie Brenner and the others. And Nettie. I thought all this would make me a better father, provide me with a better understanding of you, making it easier for me to put myself in your place.

Instead it led us to the bridge.

And beyond.

Put yourself in my place.

Or put myself in your place.

Can we strike a bargain, Ben?

Maybe if you put yourself in my place, you can see how it was.

How it was when I summoned you to the office in the middle of that terrible night . . .

I wondered how much I should tell you.

Earlier, we had awaited a decision from Washington on what our policy should be. The word that came was not unexpected. The official, public policy would be to assure the safety of the children at whatever cost the bargaining dictated. The public demanded this policy. Unofficially, our policy was to storm the bridge and rescue the children. Inner Delta had already outlined procedures for such an operation. If the attempt at rescue failed and more children were sacrificed than were saved, scapegoats had been set up to absorb the blame. They would acknowledge publicly that they went against official policy. They would be stripped of command, possibly face jail terms. The men involved were willing to assume the role of scapegoats. See what I mean about patriotism, Ben? This is the greatest patriotism: to accept disgrace for the sake of your country. The traitor as patriot. Was Judas, too, a scapegoat?

The capture of the terrorist leader known as Sedeete accelerated our plans to rescue the children. But a complication arose, one that could scuttle our plans.

One of the hijackers, the mercenary called Antibbe, was shot and killed. Accidentally. By one of the special troops: overtrained, perhaps, overzealous. Who knows? The reaction from the bridge was immediate and direct. A child was killed, the body placed on the roof of the van. But at least the bargaining continued. And your selection as the go-between was approved by the hijackers, Ben. Thus, you were summoned to my office. You were perfect for the role you had to play. Innocent of the background. Innocent of any knowledge of our plans. You were also frightened, and yet so brave, so eager to serve.

You said: "What do you want me to do, Dad? It's something to do with the bridge, isn't it? And the kids being held hostage?"

And I said: "Yes. It has to do with the bridge and the children there. An errand we want you to do. An important one."

You frowned. Yet I saw the eagerness still there in your eyes. I had to forget that you were my son. I had to resist giving you assurances. I felt that I could not deceive you to that extent. So as we talked in the office, it seemed as if I were carrying on two conversations, one with my son and the other with a member of staff personnel being given an assignment. It was important for me to remain neutral, neuter. In the service of your country it is often necessary to perform these deceits.

I told you what was involved in the assignment. That you must deliver the stone to the hijackers as proof of Sedeete's capture, to prove to the hijackers that their leader had been captured, the entire episode now pointless, that they were in no position to dictate terms but faced complete surrender at the most, negotiations at the least. I told you of the death of the second child. And the man called Antibbe.

Did you flinch? Wince? It was difficult to tell. Your eyes were watchful, alert.

"We have to play a deadly game, Ben," I said. "And as the messenger, you are caught in it. This stone they require—it may or may not be what it seems. It could be the simple proof they require that their leader is captured. Or it may be a ploy."

"What kind of ploy?"

"A ploy to deliver another hostage into their hands. Or a ploy to try to determine what our plans are—whether we are willing to negotiate or whether we plan to attack. They were careful in their selection of a messenger to deliver the stone. We suggested various people on our staff—they wanted none of them. They said they wanted a nonprofessional."

"But why is the messenger so important, Dad?"

"From their standpoint, there are several reasons. First, they want someone who will not be a threat once the messenger is with them on the bridge, in the van or the bus. Second, they would like to elicit information from the messenger, if possible. They know that we could send a messenger who is trained in deceit, programmed for action. They don't want to risk that; that's why they asked for a nonprofessional. Yet how could they know whether we were sending a nonprofessional or not? We suggested a priest—they said any man could wear a collar turned backward. We suggested some public figures whose faces were well known. They rejected this suggestion, too. They said the world was full of doubles, that our agency could probably duplicate anyone. Then I suggested you. My son. They accepted. I think they thought that a boy your age could be nothing else but what you seemed to be. And I think they also knew by the sound of my voice when I made the suggestion. The hijacker we are dealing with, the one we have deduced is the man called Artkin, said to me: 'Either you are a great patriot or a great fool.' And I replied: 'Perhaps both.' And then he accepted you."

Again, the silence. And again you waited. And then I told you: "There is a possibility, Ben, that they may question you intensively, to determine whether you are, in fact, what you appear to be. In fact, I would say it is a certainty they will question you." The key word here, of course, was *intensively*. Torture is such an old-fashioned archaic word. We avoid the term now. There are other terms. Intensive interrogation, methodological intervention, etc.

"But that's all right," you said. "You say, Dad, that I am innocent, that I don't know anything. So how could I tell them anything?"

The telephone rang at that moment. I had often pondered how our lives were altered by that call. The caller was a liaison officer from Washington, D.C., to inform me of the time chosen for our attack on the bridge. 0930 in military time. Nine thirty in the morning civilian time. I listened and made note of the time on my desk pad. I did not want to say the time aloud, not wanting you to hear it. I answered the necessary questions without unnecessary verbiage, assured the liaison that we were prepared for the action, our special forces waiting for the word.

I replaced the receiver.

I saw your eyes go to the desk pad.

Had you seen the time I had written down?

It was at that moment that I should have called it off, removed you as messenger, canceled the arrangements, picked up the telephone and told Washington I had changed my mind.

But I hesitated that fraction of a minute, and then the

door opened and the other officers came in and we were caught up in the movements bringing us to the climax of the hijacking.

The room is cold.
The heating system is even worse now than when I was a student here.

When the man called Artkin said, "Either you are a great patriot or a great fool," he knew exactly what I was. What I am. Just as I knew exactly what he was and to what lengths he would go. We knew each other across the chasm; we had recognized each other across the ravine, although we had never met.

We went by military vehicles to the scene of the bridge. You and I sat together, in the rear seat, a colonel whose name does not matter between us. At the moment you left my office, you had ceased to exist in the minds of those at Inner Delta as my son. And I know it was necessary that you had to cease to exist as my son to me for the duration of the emergency. I thought of your mother. At least she was safe in Weston. I told myself that all would go well. I wondered whether I would ever have the courage to tell her of that night, the part you and I played in it. Everything would go well, I told myself again. Artkin would receive the stone that you brought. He would also perceive that you were exactly what you seemed to be—you have an air of innocence, Ben, that cannot be denied even to a man like Artkin. There would be the inevitable questioning, however. He would inflict a degree of pain. But not much. I did not believe the pain would be excessive. Men like Artkin do not use these procedures for pleasure, for the sake of being cruel. They are professionals just as I am a professional. Expediency is the rule.

I glanced at you in the car, Ben, a swift secret glance, and saw your pale face, tension in your forehead. I had to withhold myself from reaching across the colonel to give you a pat of encouragement. You looked at me, a brief sidelong glance. I caught a glimpse of trust, determination. A look that said: I won't let you down, Dad.

The car moved through the landscape of false dawn, that reverse twilight. Only twenty miles away stood the towns of Concord and Lexington, places that had known historic moments. Your mother and I had often taken you to the Concord Bridge where the Minutemen encountered the British soldiers that April morning so long ago, a momentous explosion in our nation's history. I pondered the moment you and I were living through now. Two hundred years later in a different world. A world of assassination and terrorism, where children are pawns in deadly games. Yet I knew that if we defeated the terrorists on the bridge that morning, we would be setting a precedent for the world to see, sending a message to terrorists all over the world that our nation would not buckle under to intimidation.

When we arrived at our headquarters across the ravine from the bridge, morning light filled the scene. Morning also revealed to us the small bundle on the top of the van: the body of the child, still unidentified, who had been murdered in retaliation for the mercenary's death. We hurried you into the building so that you would not see the body immediately.

Inside, I was handed a report. The message was brief: *Communications established.*

I did not mention the report to you; it was important

that you did not know. We brought you to the window that looked out across the chasm to the bridge, the van, and the bus. You made no comment when you viewed the scene, although I saw your eyes flying everywhere.

One of the generals—his name does not matter, it is a long time since he has used his own name—outlined procedures. We would contact Artkin on the van and tell him you were on the scene. If the situation had not changed, you would be given the stone wrapped carefully and placed in a small box, half the size of a shoebox. You would walk alone the eighth-of-a-mile distance through the woods. You would wear only your shoes, socks, shorts, undershirt, and jeans. The morning would be chilly, but Artkin had insisted you wear no jacket or garment under which anything could be concealed. The box must be held out in the open at all times. Our snipers would cover you all the way.

"There has been one change," the general said, addressing me and not you. "Originally, this man Artkin said the messenger would be returned as soon as the stone was delivered. Now, he insists that he must stay until the bargaining is finished."

I had not expected that. Or had I?

"That's all right," you said, your voice small now and thin.

"It should not take long, Ben," I said. "They want to end this thing as much as we do."

You nodded, your chin firm again. I was proud of you.

We went outside while the final contact was made with Artkin. We did not wish for you to hear the contact in the event Artkin said something that could upset you.

When the signal was given, I said: "It's time, Ben."

You nodded again, still firm, resolute. The morning was chilly, but you did not shiver. Neither did I.

Nothing could touch us, I see in retrospect, except the emotions of that moment.

You said: "I don't want to let you down, Dad. I'll do my best."

"Your best is all we want, Ben. And you won't let us down, no matter what happens. I know my son."

"Time," the general said, emerging from the building.

We shook hands stiffly, Ben, you and I, although I had to resist reaching for you and enclosing you in my arms. I went inside the building. They thought it best if I did not see you make that long, vulnerable walk to the bridge. I sat down, near the monitor. I tried to keep from thinking but I knew I could not keep myself from listening. And I also knew that soon I would be listening to your voice from the van.

Communications established.

The report meant that we had managed to establish a communications link with the van without the knowledge of Artkin. One of the troopers trained in terrorist countermeasures had climbed the girders under the bridge and connected a direct line from the van to our headquarters. The connector was a sophisticated piece of equipment developed for military use. The trooper had worked painstakingly, directly under the van, under cover of darkness. The operation probably would not have been possible if there had not been space between the railroad ties for the trooper to have access to the bottom of the van. The communications device would absorb all sound within the van much like a suction cup and transmit it to our monitor in our headquarters.

I waited while you traversed the edge of the ravine in your walk to the bridge. You were part of the operation now, part of its success or failure. I did not want failure. The least of my fears was that I had volunteered to be one of the scapegoats if we met failure. The worst of my fears was you, Ben, as you made your way to the bridge. I pictured you in my mind's eye as you walked. The building I stood in was silent and so was the monitor.

But thirty minutes later, the silence would be broken by screams. Your screams.

I still hear those screams, even here in this room all this time later, screams that are as much a part of me as of you. Screams that never stop.

I know, of course, where you went when you left this room.

I said before I know you better than anyone else and I should have realized you were trying to throw me off the track when you wrote on those pages that you wouldn't go to Brimmler's Bridge until I returned to the room.

That's where you've gone.

That's where I must go.

Before it's too late.

Is it too late, Ben?

part 70

The boy was naked. Miro's first instinct was to look away. The boy looked so forlorn and pathetic and frightened that Miro did not wish to invade his privacy any further. But he also found himself fascinated by the boy who was almost a mirror to himself, except that this boy was fair with almost no body hair while Miro was dark with clusters of hair already gathered on his chest. The boy avoided Miro's eyes. His hands were crossed in front of the private place between his legs. Why was he naked?

Artkin said: "It was necessary to search him. Thoroughly." Answering Miro's unasked question. "He is clean. There was nothing hidden on him. And he brought this."

He handed Miro a gray smooth stone about the size of

an egg. Miro rubbed it with his thumb. A stone from his homeland. Would he ever see that place? It seemed so distant from this bridge, this van.

"So we know they are telling the truth," Artkin said. "They have Sedeete. But we still have the children. And this boy." He turned to the boy. "Put on your clothes." He tossed the boy his clothing, all bunched up in an untidy pile. The boy was too slow to react, and the clothing fell in a heap to the floor.

As the boy dressed himself with hurried fumbling hands, keeping his face averted, Miro studied Artkin's face. Sedeete was captured; Artkin was now in command, and Artkin liked action. Would there be action at last? But Artkin's face told him nothing. Artkin merely watched the boy dress, as if fascinated by the procedure. Miro also watched him closely. He wanted to stay alert. Artkin had summoned him here and left Stroll with the children and the girl. The best way he could serve Artkin at the moment was by being alert.

The boy was finally fully clothed. His breath came in small sharp bursts as if he had run a long distance. His hands twitched and trembled at his sides. Miro deduced that the boy was a year or two younger than himself— but then, he remembered, of course, that he did not know his own age.

"Now," Artkin said, facing the boy. "I have questions for you. And what you answer will decide whether or not you will survive. Do you understand? You must speak the truth and quickly."

The boy nodded, obviously terrified. Miro was always fascinated by the terror in people's eyes. Miro was eager for the questions and answers to begin. When Artkin had told him that a boy about his own age had been selected to deliver the stone as proof of Sedeete's capture, Miro's interest and curiosity had quickened.

But why a boy? Because, Artkin had explained, he preferred someone who was not a professional. When the general on the monitor had said he would be willing to send his own son as a gesture of goodwill, to hurry matters along and bring the bargaining closer, Artkin had been intrigued. His own son? Ordinarily, the person sent in a situation of this sort was a pawn, part of the game both sides were playing, a game in which advantages were being sought, balances were weighed. But perhaps the general was not playing a game after all. Perhaps he really wanted to bargain, unwilling to risk the death of the children. Perhaps the death of the little boy in retaliation for Antibbe's death had served a larger purpose than revenge. Who could tell about Americans, anyway? Thus, he accepted the general's son as the messenger. But he counseled Miro: "Watch him, study him. He is close to your age. You may see something that I won't see."

But all Miro could see now was this trembling, timid teen-ager.

"Tell us," Artkin said. "Are you the son of one of those generals?"

"Yes," the boy said. "My name is Ben Marchand. My father is General Mark Marchand." His voice emerged as small and thin and quavering, as if an even smaller boy inside of him were speaking.

"Tell us what you know of this entire situation and why your father chose you to bring us the stone," Artkin said, voice harsh, demanding, taking advantage of the boy's fright.

"My father called me into his office. We live on Fort Delta. He said that a package had to be delivered to the—to the men on the bridge. He said it had to be delivered by someone who could be trusted by both sides."

"Did he admit that he was placing your life in danger?"

"Yes," the boy said, gaining a bit of control now, as if his own voice were giving him courage. "He said it was risky but the risk was worth taking. He said he believed you were sincere in negotiating."

"So your father gave you the package and sent you out to us and told you nothing else?"

The boy shook his head. "Nothing."

Artkin glanced at Miro but Miro had nothing to say, nothing to ask.

"Tell me what you know of this—this affair."

"I know that you're holding the kids on the bus. It's been on radio and television. That's where I learned about it. My father's been busy all day, at Delta and out here. He came home once to see if I was all right and to tell me not to worry. They were worried at first that some of the kids whose fathers are officers at Delta might be kidnapped. He told me to stay in the house. They sent a guard to the house to watch the place."

"You stayed in your home until your father summoned you in the middle of the night?"

The boy nodded, chin trembling slightly now.

"What else did he tell you?

The boy shook his head. "Nothing." His eyes grew bright.

Miro knew that tears would come next. He felt contempt for the boy. He felt contempt for all these American boys and girls who led their selfish, unthinking lives and thought they were so smart and brave until situations developed that showed their true worth. Yet, Kate had not cried.

"Did your father say whether they were ready to bargain or whether they would attack?"

The boy shook his head again.

A pulse throbbed visibly in Artkin's temple. Miro wondered: Has he seen something I have not seen?

"It will be bad for you if we learn you are lying," Artkin said, a quiet menace in his voice. Miro knew that quietness, that menace. "We have ways of finding out about lies. You see this hand?" Artkin held up the maimed left hand, the two finger stubs evil looking in the van's dim light. "It is a crippled hand but it can still do such things to a body. A tender body like yours."

The boy flinched at the word *tender*. And the tears were very close now, gathering in the corners of his eyes but not yet spilling.

"I—I don't know—anything," he said.

"I know these generals at Fort Delta, how clever they think they are. They have sent you here for a purpose. They thought your youth would serve its purpose. How do I even know you are the son of a general? But we will find out, of course."

Artkin motioned to Miro, indicating he should go to the door of the van.

"Think about your situation for a few moments," Artkin told the boy, his voice still calm and deadly. "Think very seriously. Then we shall talk again."

He and Miro stepped out of the van into the moisture of morning. Although it had not rained, there was a patina of wetness on the tufts of grass growing through the railroad ties. Morning dew. Artkin glanced at his watch. "Seven thirty," he said. "We must wait another hour and a half."

"Even though Sedeete has been captured?" Miro asked.

"Yes," Artkin said. "My orders were to wait until nine o'clock and then take action. It doesn't matter whether

Sedeete is captured or not as far as the signal is concerned. Perhaps someone else will send it. We must wait."

"What of the boy?" Miro asked.

"He may be innocent. He may be what he appears to be—the frightened son of one of those generals. Perhaps they want to bargain. Who knows about Americans? Perhaps they cherish their children more than their agencies."

Miro said nothing. He sensed this was a time of waiting. He looked toward the bus. The tape on the windshields was like a soiled bandage. He was still astonished that the girl had tried to drive the bus from the bridge. Who would have thought she could be so daring, so brave? He frowned at the thought. But she had been foolish really to try such a thing. Stroll was now in the bus with the children and the girl. He had been reluctant to let Stroll take command of the bus: the bus was his own responsibility.

Artkin sighed, blowing air out of the corner of his mouth. A bird's cry split the air, another answered. Or were these signals? Miro looked to Artkin.

"When we go back into the van, I will apply the fingers to the boy. It will not take much to tell us whether he is not what he seems to be. If he can tell us nothing further, then we will wait for nine o'clock."

Miro wanted to ask: What then? But dared not. He had already asked Artkin more questions today than in all the time he had known him.

They crouched there a moment longer, letting the morning air caress their flesh. The bird's cries multiplied, clawing at the air. A breeze rose, shifting the bushes and brush. Were human hands assisting the breeze? How Miro wished to be away from here.

"Now, the fingers," Artkin said.

The boy cracked after thirty-two seconds. But thirty-two seconds of the fingers can be a lifetime, Miro knew. He was, in fact, surprised that the boy had resisted that long a time. He had not looked particularly brave, had seemed frightened to the point of fainting even before the fingers began. But he had held on all those seconds. Miro had ticked them off in his mind, trying to blot out the boy's screams, remembering when they had tested the fingers on each other in the classroom. Only a taste, the instructor had said. But a small taste was enough: five seconds, six, an excruciating pain that took the breath away, loosened the bowels, penetrating the deepest parts of the body.

Thirty-two seconds and then the boy, retching almost to the point of vomit, spittle in the corners of his mouth, began to talk. In small bursts, brief gasps, because the pain lingered for a moment or two after the fingers had stopped and there had to be a pause for a gathering of breath, a resting place during which the body repaired itself. And then he told them what Artkin wanted to know. The planned attack. By special forces. At nine thirty.

The boy spoke in quick, sharp spurts, tripping over words in his eagerness to talk. They are so eager to talk after the fingers, eager to show that they are cooperating, telling everything that must be known so that the fingers won't be used again. Sometimes they babble because they do not have much to say, they do not have much knowledge to impart. Like the boy. He kept repeating the same words. The telephone call. Nine thirty. Special troops. The telephone ringing in the office. Special troops. Then his voice dribbled into silence, although small sounds continued to issue from him as if he were seeking more words to tell, anything to hold off the fingers.

"Details," Artkin commanded. "Details."

The boy made a mewing sound like a small animal seeking to please its master but not knowing the master's language.

"Are they attacking by air? Will they come from under? From the ends of the bridge?"

"I don't know," the boy said, finding words now. "I don't know." His voice desperate.

And then Artkin became gentle, his old gentleness that even Miro was still unsure of.

"Take it easy," he told the boy, voice suddenly tender. "I am sorry you had to be hurt, but it was necessary. You must understand that. Now, tell me. Be calm and tell me all."

The change in Artkin's manner had an abrupt effect on the boy. He sighed, blew air out of the corner of his mouth.

"I don't know anything except what I said. They didn't tell me anything. My father said if I wasn't told anything, then I couldn't betray anything. But the telephone rang. I heard him say that the special forces were ready. I could see it was important, the way he listened to the voice on the telephone. He wrote something down. Tried to hide it with his hand. But I saw it. He had written down nine thirty. Then: A.M. after it. I pretended I didn't see it."

"What about helicopters?"

The boy shook his head.

"Will they come from under the bridge? Or either end?"

Again, a shake of the head.

"You are certain of the time?"

"Yes, yes." Eager, eager to be of service.

"It was written down?"

"Yes. Ink. A ballpoint pen."

"Are you certain you saw it clearly? Perhaps you made a mistake. Perhaps you saw it upside down and the time was six thirty." But it was already past six thirty.

Artkin said nothing more, seemed to be pondering the situation. He looked at Miro, nodding his head, a look that said he had learned the truth of the situation. The boy had told the truth. He was certain that the boy was hiding nothing. Miro knew what would happen next. It was time for the fingers again. No one could be trusted in these times. Not even children. Even children could be what they seemed not to be.

The boy read the message in Artkin's eyes, saw the reality of what had to be done. He began to whimper, cowering, his chin wobbling.

"Oh no," he said.

Miro turned away, concentrated on a dial on the monitor. The screams as usual were loud and long and lingering. Miro ticked off the seconds. Fifteen, sixteen.

The boy sagged, clutching Artkin's knees.

"What else?" Artkin said. "What else?"

Seventeen. Eighteen.

The boy could only gasp, mouth open, a fish mouth out of water, drowning in air.

"Nothing," the boy gasped, the word a strangled cry, as if torn from his insides.

"Good," Artkin said, releasing him.

Miro looked at the boy. For the first time, the boy turned his eyes to Miro. Miro had never seen such a look in anyone's eyes. Was there a word for such a look? It was beyond terror or horror or pain. A look of such anguish, such regret. As if he suddenly saw his true doom, a doom that went beyond the fingers, beyond even death. A look that left the boy hollow, empty. A look that said: What have I done? The look of the betrayer.

Miro could not look at him anymore. As he lowered his eyes, he wondered why he felt such a sense of shame, like a piece of baggage he had not meant to pick up and then found that he could not put down.

The attack came without warning.

At 8:35.

A moment before the attack began, Kate was wiping the nose of a child who was quietly crying for her mother. Artkin was sitting in the van, dozing. But not really dozing; this was a trick of his, to rest, to replenish his strength, sitting with arms dangling loosely, eyes half closed. Stroll sat in the doorway of the van, alert as usual, looking down, studying the space between the railroad ties at his feet, trying to spot activity down there. The boy sat on the floor of the van, his back against the rear door, staring ahead with dull eyes or perhaps not staring at all but contemplating something unseen, invisible in the cluttered van, invisible but terrible. This was how Miro had seen them all a moment before the attack, having gone to the van to ask Artkin if he was certain there were no more drugs because the children were becoming restless again and Kate was not useful any longer. Since the little boy had been shot, she was like a sleepwalker, going through the motions, her actions and reactions mechanical, as if drugged like the children had been earlier. Artkin had shaken his head without breaking his concentration, and Miro had sighed, stepping over Stroll to return to the bus. In the bus, he started to reapply a strip of tape that had come loose from a window.

Miro did not react immediately to the strange sound that reached his ears. The sound was a *whoosh*, not an explosion but a muffled eruption of noise close by the bus. He would have reacted instantly to gunfire, a grenade bursting, the whine of a sniper's rifle. He paused, listening. There was only silence. He returned to his work, lulled by what the naked boy had said: the attack would come at 9:30. But one half hour too late, according to Artkin's plan. Then, another *whoosh*, this time enveloping the bus, and the bus seemed to move slightly, the way a great ship might lurch as it bumps into a pier. Miro reached for his pistol and ran toward the doorway.

The doorway was shrouded in sudden fog. He fumbled with the lock, opened the door. The fog swirled into the doorway, heavy, thick, clinging and moist. A chemical stung Miro's eyeballs.

"Artkin," Miro cried.

The gunfire started. More than gunfire. Explosions, the quick stutter of machine guns. Sirens. The throbbing of a helicopter; two perhaps. Detonations that shook the bus. An orchestra of chaos, deafening to the ears, jarring the senses. Miro withdrew from the doorway and turned toward Kate. She was only a few feet away, her eyes suddenly alert, alive. Do not trust her, he told himself, remembering how she had tried to drive the bus to freedom. But he needed her now. She could get him out of here. The attack was on. The naked boy had fooled them, fooled Artkin, and now they must fight the enemy's fight and not theirs.

"Kate," Miro yelled, brandishing his automatic. He raced to her. The children were screaming, but their voices were barely audible in the din surrounding them. Miro thrust the gun into Kate's ribs, saw her wince, jammed it further. "Stay with me. A false move and I shoot and you are dead." He pushed her to the doorway.

The winds had started. The turbulent winds of the helicopter's blades were dispersing the fog, tearing it to shreds, as if the fog had been a massive cotton blanket. Pieces of the cotton drifted in the air. Miro tore strips of tape from the windshield. He had to see what was going on outside the bus without leaving it. The bus would be safe for the next few moments at least. The soldiers knew the children were in the bus and would not fire into it or toss grenades inside. But they would have to enter sooner or later, and Miro knew he had to be out of here. He looked through the windshield, through the patches of clear space left by the dispersing fog. He saw Stroll's body on the tracks at the entrance of the van. His body was curled up, his arms clutching his chest. Miro knew he was dead: the attitude of a dead body is unmistakable. Antibbe, now Stroll. What of Artkin? But Artkin had the boy, just as Miro had Kate.

Miro stepped to the door, Kate still beside him, the gun still in her ribs. A soldier loomed before them, the doorway empty one moment and then filled with the soldier the next moment. The soldier seemed to erupt from the ear-splitting noise that assaulted them, seemed to be part of it all. The soldier held a grenade in his hand; Miro knew that grenade: the kind they called the stun grenade. The stun grenade did not throw shrapnel—it knocked out anyone caught in its concussion, knocked them out for a short time but long enough for an enemy to take over. Miro could not let the grenade explode. He raised his gun but before he could fire the soldier suddenly crumpled and fell backward, the grenade flung from his hand onto the tracks. Looking through the windshield again, Miro saw Artkin at the door of the van, revolver in one hand, holding the limp boy in the other. Artkin had saved him. Again.

Miro pushed the girl down the steps of the bus to the outside. Sooner or later, they would invade the bus and he had to get out. Just as Artkin had left the van. Each had his hostage: their tickets to freedom. Let them have the children. He had Kate, and Kate would die before he did.

The chemical fog rolled in heavy again, the patches of cotton dancing madly now in the winds caused by the helicopter blades. Miro's eyes darted toward both ends of the bridge and saw nothing. Where were the attackers? He looked to Artkin, and Artkin, too, looked puzzled. The noise of the rotors increased. Miro looked up and and saw the ski-like foot of a helicopter stabbing through the swirling fog. Were they going to land here on the bridge? On the top of the bus, crazy as that would be? Or would they come from below? His eyes darted to the tracks, but his feet were shrouded in fog. He clutched the girl with one hand, continued to prod her with the gun. But she did not struggle. She might have been sobbing; he could not hear above the noise. He looked to Artkin, needing answers. What now? Where is the enemy? When is he coming? And as he looked, he saw them at last, at the far end of the bridge, five or six of them, advancing with rifles ready, clad in camouflaged uniforms, beyond Artkin, beyond the van. Miro opened his mouth to shout a warning to Artkin but knew his voice could not be heard. Artkin was studying the helicopter that was emerging from the fog above them. Miro withdrew the gun from the girl's ribs, intending to catch Artkin's attention by waving frantically or moving toward him. But the girl, at the release of the gun's pressure from her body, burst forward. Miro grabbed at her; he could not risk losing her and thus lose his chance to get out of here. He pulled her back to him, close, their bodies crushed together. He turned again to Artkin and saw Artkin stiffen, saw his arms grow rigid, saw the cords in his neck bulge as if small worms crept beneath his flesh. Miro knew Artkin was shot but he saw no blood, saw only the familiar body suddenly become the body of a stranger. Artkin's grip on the boy loosened, and the boy spun away from him, gathering his arms across his chest as if to protect himself. Artkin's body swiveled, still stiff, his head turning with his body as though he were standing on a turntable, a turntable slowly revolving. Artkin's hand, holding the gun, extended itself. His arm jerked backward as the gun fired. Miro saw the bullet penetrate the boy's flesh, saw the crimson badge appear on the boy's chest. The boy fell, eyes glazed, body rigid, mouth frozen. Artkin, too, fell, dropping the gun. As he fell, he faced Miro and his eyes were already sightless. His mouth was a hole through which blood gushed, but blood like Miro had never seen before, thick and dark, as if Artkin's tongue had swollen a thousand times and then exploded in shreds from his mouth. Miro was held: Artkin dead. He had never counted on Artkin dying, only himself and the others.

It was at that moment that the helicopter crashed into the roof of the van in a blast of flame and smoke, the shock of the explosion sending both Miro and the girl reeling from the doorway of the bus, flinging them onto the tracks, five or six feet away. Miro clung to the girl, knowing instinctively that he could not let her go, could not lose her in the smoke and the rubble and the chaos that surrounded them. Miro's eyes hurt and his lungs burned. As he and the girl tumbled together in the rubble and the debris, dust mingling with the fog close to the ground, he was aware of soldiers everywhere around them but moving past them as if he and the girl were invisible. Shouts penetrated the noise now: *Christ, the chopper hit the van.* . . . *Get that guy out of there.* . . . *Check the kids.* Miro scrambled to his feet. He helped Kate to her feet, but she resisted, trying to pull away from him, defiance in her eyes. He looked toward the end of the bridge and realized, astonishingly, that it was unguarded: it was a clear means of escape to the woods, out of this hell of fire and smoke and fog. The helicopter crash had distracted the soldiers; their concern for the children had also caused them to ignore Miro and the girl. All the activity was centered on the scene of the crash.

"Come," Miro said, brandishing the gun, waving it toward the woods. He pushed her and she staggered forward. As Miro started after her, a searing pain shot through the calf of his left leg. He looked down to see blood staining his pants. A bullet? A piece of shrapnel? A cut sustained when he was thrown by the explosion? He clenched his teeth against the pain and thrust himself after Kate, the gun in her ribs and his other hand on her shoulder, not so much to prevent her from escaping now but for support. The pain was excruciating; he wanted to cry out. But he could not let the girl see him that way. She would take advantage, break free.

Stumbling, struggling, they reached the end of the bridge. The fog lay heavy here, undisturbed by the helicopter blades. The fog stung their eyes again. Miro looked back, squinting through the fog. Both the helicopter and the van were enveloped in flame and smoke, the blades of the helicopter jutting into the sky like the broken wings of a wounded bird. The bus was untouched. Soldiers were piling into the bus. The children were safe. But not Artkin. Artkin was dead, Artkin who was worth more than all the children.

"Move, move," Miro whispered furiously to Kate. "Into the woods."

Miro's voice was odd in his ears, like the voice of a stranger.

They were huddled so closely together that their breaths mingled as if in some weird kind of artificial respiration: Kate could not tell where her breath left off and Miro's began. Her thighs were soaked with urine—her bladder had given way completely during the attack—and perspiration bathed the rest of her body. Not perspiration—sweat. Sweat that came from deep inside her, heavy and musky. Or was it Miro's sweat? She knew it was Miro's blood that had splashed on her jeans, blood from the gash in his leg. He had torn his pants and exposed the wound: torn tissue quietly pulsing blood. She knew he felt the pain. She could see it in his eyes. His breathing had an extra dimension, an extra depth. Her breath came in exhausted gasps, from running and struggling with Miro as they'd made their way through the woods. But Miro's breathing had more than exhaustion in it. He was gulping air and his breaths came fast, faster than Kate's. She looked down at the pulsing blood and thought: Maybe I can get away at last, maybe the wound will spill his blood away.

They were in a small nestlike enclosure Miro had spotted in the woods, a haven of bushes and fallen branches, probably some child's abandoned fort. Kate remembered how she liked to sneak into small places when she was a kid and hide from the world. She and Miro were hiding now. The place did not accommodate two people, barely one. They were joined together in a ferocious embrace. Miro had shoved her into the enclosure first, and she thought he was leaving her there because there was room only for herself. Then he had climbed in as well, pushing and squirming, keeping the revolver always aimed at her somehow. She had to bend and twist her body to allow him entry. Now they were locked together, legs entwined, faces only inches apart, mouths almost exhaling into each other and the gun still wedged between them, below her left breast, hurting her, bruising her ribcage. Her fear was that the gun would go off accidentally. Her heart beat in heavy thuds. Or was it Miro's? In the distance she could hear the sound of shouting, faint sounds, like a radio playing with the volume turned to low.

She sighed, weary, dispirited. But knew she had to begin somewhere, sometime.

"You can't get away," she said. "We're surrounded." Speaking was an effort and her voice emerged as if she were talking in a huge cavern.

"Be quiet," Miro said, his voice a rasp, hoarse, strangled.

At least the children were safe, Kate thought. At least? No, not least. The children had been the important ones from the beginning. And now they were safe, rescued, probably being handed over to their mothers and fathers at this moment. How about my mother and father? How about me? Yeah, how about me?

She had to avoid panic. She had to concentrate on the positive side of things. She couldn't give up now. When the smoke cleared on the bridge and everything calmed down, they'd search the woods. Miro would never be able to escape. Not alone. Not in these woods that were unknown to him.

"My ankle hurts," Kate said. "I twisted it just before we stopped running. A bad twist. Maybe it's sprained. I'll be a drag on you. Why don't you leave me here? You can make it faster alone."

She was amazed at her ability to lie, to improvise, to plot and scheme. Yet there was no one to see how cunning she could be. If Miro could see, then it would come to no good. She thought of the bus and all those hours she'd tried to hang on. Had she done well? Had she been brave enough? She'd botched up the escape attempt. She wished she could talk to somebody about it, maybe her mother and father, and they'd say, the way they always said when she'd attempted something and failed: Well, at least you tried, Kate. That was something, wasn't it? Maybe she hadn't been brave, but at least she'd tried, hadn't she? She wished there were somebody here to tell her yes. She had never felt so lonely in all her life, a desperate kind of loneliness with a sadness in it.

"You will stay with me, Kate. Without you, they would shoot me like a dog," Miro said. His breathing was more regular now, his voice almost normal. He pushed the gun deeper into her ribs. "I will shoot you if I have to, Kate. My orders from the beginning were to shoot you. Kill you. I would not hesitate now."

She regarded him with horror. But she couldn't let him see the horror. "Why didn't you shoot me, then?"

"We needed you. To take care of the children. But Artkin said I would have my chance before we left the bridge." He was breathing hard again and grimacing against the pain.

She had been right. She had seen her doom in their eyes. She raised her eyes to Miro now, knowing her doom was still there. He looked down at his leg. "The blood, it's stopping," he said.

"Even if it stops, what good will it do?" Kate said, summoning all that was left in her to play the role, keep him talking, reach him again as she had reached him once or twice on the bus. But, God, she was tired.

"No more words, Kate, no more games."

"I'm not playing games. Look at the facts. You're hurt. The woods are full of soldiers. You're in a strange country. There's no way out."

He didn't respond. She pressed on. "Look, maybe if you give yourself up, they'll go easy on you. After all, you didn't do anything. You didn't kill Raymond. The kids are safe. Even the first one who died, little Kevin McMann, that was an accident. I'll testify in your behalf. I'll tell them you were kind to the children. To me. You didn't hurt us. You didn't do anything."

His lips arranged themselves in a smile. But a smile without mirth, without depth, just an arrangement of flesh. "Ah, Kate. You have missed the entire point. All of it. All the times we talked on the bus and you still do not understand."

"Understand what?"

"That it does not matter whether or not I get away. Whether or not I live or die. Whether anyone else lives or dies. I have served my purpose."

His voice was strong and determined now, and she had to fight that strength and that determination.

"What purpose? What the hell has purpose got to do with living or dying?" How could she get through, pierce his defenses, penetrate this propaganda he'd been fed all these years? She remembered how he had looked at her that time on the bus when she'd taken off her jeans. And she felt ashamed at what she must attempt again. Christ, did it always have to come down to that between a boy and a girl, a man and a woman?

She tried to make her voice tender. "How about all the things you could do in this world? Don't you want love? Get married? Have children? What's wrong with a little love? Instead of death and fighting, and that war you're always talking about."

He stared at her, eyes blank. Her body sagged. What she was talking about—love, children, family—was beyond his comprehension. Even sex, maybe. She realized again how innocent he was in the most terrible sense of innocence: the innocence of a monster. But she had to persist.

"All right, then, what have you got? What good would it do you to escape? You're alone. Alone in the world out there. Those two men who were with you are dead, the one you called Antibbe and the black guy. And Artkin. Who's left? Nobody. Your brother's dead. And now your father."

He looked at her, startled. His breath, stale and rancid, entered her mouth, her nostrils. "My father— what do you mean? *Now* my father?"

When she had spoken the words, she didn't realize the knowledge they contained, knowledge she had somehow absorbed earlier, knowledge she didn't even know she had until it emerged, like having an answer to a hard test at school after having forgotten how or when you learned it. Now, the possibility of Artkin being Miro's father blossomed fully and also the awareness that Miro didn't know, had never suspected. Actually, even Kate doubted it. Could it be true? And could she use the knowledge to her advantage?

"Artkin. He *was* your father, wasn't he?" she said, watching him closely, gauging his reaction.

"What makes you say that? You know nothing of us."

"You look like father and son," Kate said, improvising, thoughts scurrying. And then she saw the truth: "When I saw you in the masks, that first time, I knew. Your lips, your eyes—both the same. I wondered why you didn't call him father."

"It's not possible," Miro cried out, trying to turn away from her. But there was no place to go, no way he could escape her or her words.

"Why not?" Kate said, telling herself to keep talking, keep on going. She had drawn blood again, gained time, caught him off guard, off balance again. "Didn't you say he found you in the camps and brought you to that school? Would a stranger do that? Maybe he'd been looking for you and your brother all those years. Why did he take you to a place where you'd be safe, taken care of? And why did he come back for you later? Would he have done all that if he wasn't your father? If he was just a stranger?"

"My father died. With my mother. Long ago. When a mine exploded," Miro insisted, but there was doubt in his voice now.

"But you didn't see them die. Somebody told your brother and your brother told you."

Artkin his father? He could not acknowledge that truth, if it were truth. Because there was a worm crawling in his heart, a worm that said he had been responsible for Artkin's death. He had betrayed Artkin, had reached for the girl instead of warning him of the approaching soldiers on the bridge. He had chosen the girl and his own safety over Artkin, Artkin who had been everything to him and now even his father.

A cry rose out of him, from the depths of his being, a cry that went beyond sorrow and pain and anguish, flowing from the body as blood must flow from a wound. The sound enveloped Kate so that she became part of his cry. He lifted his face from hers. His head thrown back, he wailed at the air the way an animal mortally wounded must announce its final desperate moments.

Kate cradled him, moving one free arm to embrace him. His wailing formed a word now as it rose from the hiding place, bursting out of the enclosure. *Aaaarrtt-kinnnnnnn!* Rising and then dying in the air, lingering as only a faint echo in the ears. Kate rocked him gently, the way she had rocked the children on the bus, crooning softly, a song without a tune, words without meaning, but sounds to bring him comfort and solace. She closed her eyes, enfolding him, enclosing him with her body, with her warmth and her breath, her sweat and her urine.

When he squeezed the trigger, the bullet smashed her heart, and she was dead within seconds.

When Kate Forrester was nine years old, she almost choked to death. A chunk of meat caught in her throat. For one terrible moment, she was stiff with terror, her throat jammed with the meat, unable to move, her breath cut off so swiftly and completely between inhale and exhale that she could not even gasp, but could only try to rise to her feet, eyes bulging, mouth frozen open. She could not move, could not utter a sound, was paralyzed, silent, and thought: I am dying and nobody knows although they're here at the table with me, my mother and father. And then at the moment when suffocation threatened, and the room began to grow dim and far away, the lodged meat somehow, miraculously, loosened. And she coughed and retched, and the meat came up into her mouth, freeing her, unlocking her bones and muscles, allowing the air to rush into her lungs, and she was instantly bathed in a cool perspiration that glistened on her skin. With the breath came a sense of reprieve, the sweet knowledge that she was not going to die after all, she was going to live. Life, the act of being alive and able to draw breath, was suddenly unbearably beautiful, like music within her. She was safe. Safe.

But not this time.

This time, everything had stopped the way a watch stops, and the pain was her body and her body was the pain and she knew exactly what had happened and was going to happen. The gun had gone off. She was caught again between inhale and exhale. The pain . . . wow . . . breath-caught dying mommy and daddy I can't breathe and nobody to tell me if I was bra . . .

part 77

Hello, Dad.

Ben, you're here. You're back.

Yes, I'm here. You've been looking for me, haven't you?

For so long, Ben.

How long, Dad? Weeks? Months?

Too long, much too long.

But I was always here. Didn't you know that, Dad?

Sometimes I thought you were.

You just didn't look long enough or deep enough.

I tried, Ben.

Did you try hard enough?

I did everything I could, Ben.

Did you really want to bring me back?

Yes, of course.

Maybe you were fooling yourself. Or fooling me. Or is there a difference?

Don't play games, Ben.

I'm not playing games, Dad. I'm just wondering if you really wanted to bring me back. I came back before.

But I didn't know.

Yes, you knew. Look at the papers there, near the typewriter. You see? That was me.

But I didn't see you. I only saw the papers.

I had to leave, but now I'm back again.

And I'm glad, Ben, glad.

Don't you want to know where I've been?

You don't have to tell me, Ben.

Because you already know, don't you?

Don't say that, Ben.

I want you to say it.

Say what?

Where I've been. Where I've come back from.

But I can't say it.

Yes, you can.

I don't want to say it.

Too bad, too bad. It took so long to bring me back. All that time. All that time staring out the window and all that time awake at night when even the pills didn't put you to sleep. All that time and now you don't want to say it.

I can't say it.

Yes, you can. Try, at least.

Why should I?

Because you owe me that much. Now tell me where I've come from.

All right, then.

From where?

Me. From me.

Where in you?

Deep inside.

So deep it was hard to bring me back, wasn't it?

Yes, it was hard.

But now I'm here, aren't I?

Please go back, Ben. Go back.

But I just got here. And it took so long, so long to bring me back. But now I'm here. And you're here. At last.

Go back, Ben.

But why should I go back when you tried so hard to bring me here?

Because I'm tired, Ben. So tired.

Why did you want to bring me back, Dad?

You know why, Ben. You know.

Do I?

Yes.

But tell me. I want to hear you say it.

I wanted to ask you to forgive me. For what I did to you. On the bridge.

And what did you do?

I was serving my country. I am a patriot, Ben. I did it for my country. Not for myself.

I know you did it for your country, Dad. But I'm your son. And I love you.

But tell me what you did for your country.

I sent you to the bridge. To the van. It was a vital situation and you were the choice.

Why me, Dad? Why not someone else?

Because I knew you better than anyone else. I knew what would happen at the bridge, what you'd do.

And what would I do, Dad?

I already told you. At the hospital. Remember?

Yes, but tell me again. That's why I'm here, isn't it?

I went to the hospital to visit you. You had been unconscious since the attack on the bridge. The bullet had pierced your arm, penetrated your chest. We, your mother and I, visited every day. And then one day you emerged from the coma. We were alone, you and I. You spilled on your cheeks. I bent close to you. I had never loved you as much as at that moment. You started to speak. You said you were sorry. Sorry that you had told them about the attack. The attack at nine thirty. You said you were sorry you had let me down, let your country down, had not been brave enough. I took you in my arms. I told you that you should not be sorry, that you had been brave. As brave as you were able to be. Nobody, not even your country, could ask for more. I said that you were supposed to tell them that the attack would come at nine thirty. It had been planned that way. You were selected for that purpose. We needed someone who would tell them what they wanted to hear. The telephone call while you were in my office was planned. So was the desk pad and the time I wrote down for you to see. We wanted you to hear the telephone conversation about special forces. To see the time on the pad. So that you could tell them and so that they would believe you. So that we could attack earlier. Take them by surprise and save the children.

But what about me?

We didn't anticipate that they would not release you. We didn't anticipate that Artkin would have time to shoot you. It was computerized as a minimum risk.

I don't mean that.

What do you mean?

I mean: what about me? To find out that I not only betrayed my country but had been expected to do it. To find out that I was expected to act as a coward, unable to take a little pain.

It was a lot of pain. More than we computed. A lot of others would have cracked.

But I was the one who cracked. I was expected to crack. Whether the pain was bad or not, you knew I'd crack. You counted on me being a coward.

Not a coward.

What was I then?

Vulnerable.

A coward.

Susceptible.

A coward.

You were serving your country. Serving it in your way just as I was serving it in mine.

Is a country worth that much, Dad? How could I have gone through life knowing what I had done? Knowing that my cowardice had served my country. Where did that leave me, Dad?

I'm sorry, Ben. I was sorry as soon as I told you. As soon as I saw your face and realized what I had done. I thought: I'll make it up to you. If it takes months, years. I'll earn your forgiveness.

And then I died.

Oh, Ben.

Another bridge, another day.

I tried to stop you, Ben.

But you were too late, weren't you?

I failed you. Again.

But I couldn't have gone on living anyway, could I?

No.

And you buried me.

Yes.

Twice.

Yes.

Once in the ground, in the military cemetery at Fort Delta. And again inside of you. Buried me deep inside of you.

Yes. I tried to forget, to escape.

But you keep bringing me back.

I know. To tell you I'm sorry, to ask your forgiveness.

Then why not ask me?

Because I'm afraid.

Afraid of what?

It's hard for me to say it.

Let me say it for you. You're afraid that I won't forgive you.

Yes.

That's why you keep bringing me back and then making me go.

Yes.

Then let me say it.

Will you?

Yes. I'll say it. I forgive you.

Thank you, Ben.

See? I said it. Now you won't have to send me back again. Now I can stay.

But I think you should go, Ben.

I like it here. It's nice. It's like your old prep school, Castleton, isn't it? And the doctor. Doesn't he remind you of Dean Albertson? You told me all about him. How he talked so much, always rambling on.

I think you ought to go now, Ben.

And the others. Your old friends, Martingale and Donateli. They're still here, aren't they? In your yearbook. Knights and Dayze.

I want you to go, Ben.

And Nettie Halversham. We're all mixed up about her, aren't we? I told you about her, didn't I? Or did you overhear me talking about her? Is she mine or yours? Did you know a girl like her once?

Please, Ben, stop.

No. I don't think I'll stop. And I won't leave, either. You once said, "Put yourself in my place, Ben." Well, that's exactly what I'm doing, Dad.

You can't.

Why can't I?

Because you can't stay.

Oh yes I can.

You cannot.

But I like it here.
You must go.
I think I'll stay.
I order you to go.
Tell you what, Dad.
What?
You go.
I must stay.
That's it. You go.
No, I can't go.
Why not?
I won't go.
Yes, you will.
Please, Ben.
You brought me here but that doesn't mean you can send me away. You brought me back before and made me leave. But this time I'm staying.
No, you can't. You mustn't.
This time you're going. Not me.
I can't.
Yes, you can.
I won't.
Yes, you will.
No.
You'd better go now, Dad.
No . . .
You can't stay any longer.
Please . . .
I'm here to stay.
No . . .

Good-bye, Dad.

part
12

The rain had stopped but the pavement was still wet. Despite the rain, the day had remained warm. Now that evening was here, the heat and humidity were high. Miro's clothes were soaked. The clothing stuck to his flesh. The rain had begun in mid-afternoon, had shortly reached a crescendo, the clouds like broken dams, and then abated. Miro had kept moving through the downpour, knowing he could not indulge in the luxury of rest or recuperation. He kept low to the ground, darting and scurrying from bush to shrub to tree. He had climbed trees twice to elude his pursuers. Once, he had removed his undershirt, torn it into strips that he used to bandage his injured leg. He became immune to the pain. Or perhaps his entire body was so pain-wracked that he could not tell where he began and the pain left off. He was neither hungry nor thirsty. He felt neither weak nor strong. He simply existed.

He was sitting in bushes by the side of the highway. Darkness had fallen. The lights of passing cars stabbed at the darkness. He wondered whether he should chance hitching a ride. He sensed danger in it. Miro knew that his description had probably been circulated throughout the area, throughout the state and nation. He also knew that he looked a sight, soaked and bloody.

He glanced over his shoulder. The woods were dark and silent. A stench rose to his nostrils. His own stench. He had swum through a river thick with scum to escape the searchers. The river ran beside several old factories and by a dump. He thought of his pursuers, the close calls he'd had. It had been like a game but he had taken no pleasure in it. He had used the knowledge he had gained in the camps and the training school, relying on instinct as well.

Once, he'd wondered: Why am I running? Why do I wish to escape? He should have died with Artkin on the bridge. That would have been a statement for others to see. Then he remembered all the lessons Artkin had taught him, day by day, year by year. He realized Artkin had taught him for a purpose. It would have been glorious to die with Artkin on the bridge. But it was more important to carry on the work. So Miro had persisted in his escape, willing himself to continue past pain and exhaustion.

Traffic was light now. Cars passed only occasionally. A truck lumbered into view and vanished in the night. The highway was dark, without streetlights. Miro sensed that the darkness was a friend, that he should take advantage of the night to get away from here. He needed to get to Boston; once there, he could hide in a dozen places and then make contacts. The best way to go would be in one of the passing cars or trucks. The solution was simple: hitch a ride, then kill the driver, dump the body somewhere, and continue on his way. The gun was still in his belt, fully loaded except for the bullet he had spent on the girl.

He thought of the girl. And Artkin. And his last sight of them. Artkin dying as he fell. The girl curled up in the bushes, her face hidden. Both his victims. He knew he had killed Artkin by reaching for the girl instead of warning him of the approaching soldiers. He was responsible for Artkin's death. Thus, Artkin had been his first death, not the girl. And the girl. She had been playing games with him, the way she had played games with him on the bus. It was impossible that Artkin was his father. For one moment, the girl had made him believe it. The moment had pierced him with—what? Something. Like the something he had known when she touched his arm on the bus. He remembered how her flesh glowed in the dimness of the bus. He had been filled with that something he could not put a name to. The girl had asked him once: Don't you feel anything? Perhaps he had been filled with feeling at that moment. He did not know. He did not care. He would not let himself be filled with anything again. He would keep himself empty, like before.

A car stopped nearby. A station wagon. The driver got out of the car. A man, short and fat. The man looked around and began to walk toward the woods at the edge of the roadway, fumbling with his trousers, apparently seeking a place to urinate. Miro recognized his good fortune. He decided he would not waste a bullet but would use his hands.

He moved out of the bushes into the world that was waiting for him.